mary-kateandashley
so little time

Check out these other great
so little time
titles:

Book 1: **how to train a boy**

Book 2: **instant boyfriend**

Book 3: **too good to be true**

Book 4: **just between us**

Book 5: **tell me about it**

Book 6: **secret crush**

Book 7: **girl talk**

Book 8: **the love factor**

Book 9: **dating game**

Book 10: **a girl's guide to guys**

Coming soon!

Book 12: **best friends forever**

mary-kateandashley
so little time

boy crazy

by Megan Stine

Based on the screenplay by Randi Barnes

≡HarperCollins*Entertainment*
An Imprint of HarperCollins*Publishers*

A PARACHUTE PRESS BOOK

A PARACHUTE PRESS BOOK

Parachute Publishing, L.L.C.
156 Fifth Avenue
Suite 325
NEW YORK
NY 10010

First published in the USA by HarperEntertainment 2003
First published in Great Britain by HarperCollins*Entertainment* 2004
HarperCollins*Entertainment* is an imprint of HarperCollins*Publishers* Ltd,
77-85 Fulham Palace Road, Hammersmith, London W6 8JB

The HarperCollins website address is
www.harpercollins.co.uk

1 3 5 7 9 10 8 6 4 2

The authors assert the moral right to be
identified as the authors of the work.

ISBN 0 00 714456 3

Printed and bound in Great Britain by Clays Ltd, St Ives plc

chapter
one

"Tell me it isn't true, Lennon," fourteen-year-old Chloe Carlson said into the phone. She was lying on her bed, talking to her boyfriend, Lennon Porter. "Tell me you don't have to work the entire winter break."

"I don't know," Lennon replied, "but I have to work today. In fact, I'm supposed to be there right now. I'll e-mail you later, okay?"

"Okay." Chloe sighed as she hung up the phone. Lennon worked at the Newsstand, a cool coffee bar and Internet café with computer terminals all over the place.

Sure. E-mail me. Like that's going to do any good! Chloe thought. Just a few minutes ago she'd been reading through her old e-mails from Lennon. They were all the same. She'd write, *Want to go to a movie?* and he'd write back, *Can't. Gotta work tonight.*

There were ten just like that. Eleven, if you counted the e-mail he wrote *from* work. It said, *Chloe.*

Wish I were anywhere but here — *with you*. It was signed, *Lennon the Latte-Meister*.

Why am I complaining? she wondered.

After all, Lennon was by far the smartest and most interesting guy she'd ever dated. He was cute and honest and funny, too. But lately he was winning in the "Best Boyfriend Who's Never Around for a Date" category.

If he works all week, this vacation is going to be the worst, she thought. With another sigh, she hopped off the bed, brushed her long blonde hair out of her face, and went downstairs to see what her twin sister, Riley, was doing.

Riley was sitting in the living room with their mother, Macy. The two of them were hunched over a magazine.

"What's up?" Chloe asked, joining them.

"Mom's going nuts about some movie star," Riley answered. "Are you sure he's famous, Mom? I've never heard of him."

Macy Carlson's mouth dropped open. "Are you kidding? He's a major star! I can't believe you've never heard of Jacques D'Oisseau! Are you sure you're my daughter?"

Riley glanced at Chloe and faked a gasp. "Oh, no! Maybe we were switched at birth!"

"Very funny," Macy said, smirking.

Chloe reached for the magazine and stared at a photo of a French actor. He had dark eyes, a classic tan, and wavy silver hair. "What's the big deal about this Jacques guy?"

"He rented the house right down the beach from us," Macy replied. "I saw him move in yesterday."

"Oh." Chloe tossed the magazine back to her mom.

"I can't believe you aren't more excited!" Macy said.

Chloe shrugged. "Sorry, Mom, but we don't speak much French yet. We've only been taking it a few months in school."

"Besides," Riley chimed in, "he's almost as old as Manuelo."

"I heard that!" Manuelo announced from the kitchen in his Spanish accent. Manuelo Del Valle was a full-time housekeeper and cook for the Carlsons. He had been with them forever – from even before Chloe and Riley's parents had separated. He carried a tray of bagels and juice into the living room and set it down.

"You hear *everything*," Chloe teased him. "You must have the biggest ears in the house."

"Believe it," Manuelo joked, pretending to be proud of them. "And by the way, my little lemonade, how dare you say that I'm as old as Jacques D'Oisseau? He is at least five years older. Maybe ten!"

Manuelo snatched the magazine from Macy and stared at the photo. "I can only hope I look that good when I am his age," he declared.

[Chloe: Yawn. Sorry, but I can't get worked up about some old French guy. Even if he IS a movie star. I'm just wondering what I'm going to do now that winter break is here. So far it looks like it's going to be boring, boring, boring. Now if you told me that some YOUNG, hot actor moved into the house next to ours, THAT might be worth getting pumped about.]

"Did you know that he's shooting a commercial here in Malibu?" Manuelo went on.

[Chloe: A commercial? Okay, maybe THAT'S worth getting pumped about.]

"Where?" Chloe asked, perking up.

"At your favourite hang-in," Manuelo said.

"Hangout," Chloe corrected him. "You mean the Newsstand?"

"That's the place," Manuelo said.

Chloe was suddenly interested. "What kind of commercial?"

"It's some kind of coffee thing for the Superbowl," Manuelo said. "I read about it in the newspaper. Jacques is getting too old for leading man roles, so he's going to focus on directing instead. Including this major commercial."

"Cool! Maybe I can watch them filming!" Chloe announced.

"I wouldn't mind watching them shoot it, either," Riley said. "I mean, we don't have anything better to do this week."

"Sorry, my little lemonades." Manuelo shook his head. "The set will probably be closed."

"Maybe Lennon can get us in?" Riley suggested.

"It's worth a try," Manuelo said.

"Yeah," Chloe agreed. "Why not? We've got to do *something* to kick off this winter break."

Riley made a quick phone call to her friend Sierra Pomeroy and arranged to meet her at the Newsstand.

Twenty minutes later she and Chloe pushed open the glass doors to the coffee house. A bunch of little tables and chairs filled the centre of the room. Along one wall was a rack of international newspapers. Another wall was lined with computers. And at the back was a small stage for performers.

"Sierra!" Riley called, seeing her friend head into the rest room. Riley hurried to catch up with her. "Wow," she said, checking out the checked skirt and boring white shirt Sierra was wearing. "Your mom makes you dress like that even for *break*?"

Sierra nodded and shrugged. She pulled off her scrunchie, letting her flaming red hair fall around her shoulders. "Whatever. It'll be all gone in a sec," she said, gesturing at her clothes.

Sierra's real name was Sarah, but only her teachers and her parents called her that. Everyone else knew the truth – that she was leading a double life.

so little time

At home she wore conservative clothes, played the violin and went by the name her parents had given her. But the minute she was off her mother's radar, she changed into totally hip outfits and let down her hair. Then she became the person she wanted to be – Sierra, bass guitar player in a rock band called The Wave.

Riley watched as Sierra balled up the skirt and shirt and stuffed them into her backpack. Quickly she slipped into a pair of mango-coloured silk cargo pants and a lime green top.

"This is getting to be a major chore," Sierra said, nodding towards the backpack with the extra clothes. "I'm so over living a double life."

"How come?" Riley was surprised. "I thought you sort of liked the whole drama of it."

Sierra shook her head. "For one thing, look at these trousers! They're so wrinkled, it looks as if I've been sleeping in a mummy case."

"Wrinkled is in," Riley argued.

"Maybe," Sierra sighed. "But it's more than that. I'm running out of excuses to tell my mom every time I have to go practise with the band."

Plus it must be weird not being able to tell your parents the truth about anything, Riley thought. She would hate having to lie to her parents all the time.

"Hey," Riley said. "What if you told them?"

"Huh?" Sierra blinked as she applied some black eyeliner.

"I don't know. It's just an idea, but what if you told your parents the whole story?" Riley suggested. "About your band, your name, your taste in wrinkled clothing…"

"Ha-ha. Very funny," Sierra said.

"No, I'm serious," Riley insisted. "Why not? I mean, what have you got to lose?"

"What have I got to lose?" Sierra's eyes opened wide. "Are you kidding? They could make me stop playing guitar altogether."

"That would be bad," Riley admitted. "But what are the chances? Your parents aren't the worst humans on the planet or anything. They're just—"

"Strict? Old-fashioned? Demanding? And totally convinced they know what's best for me?" Sierra said, filling in the gap. "Pick any two."

"Okay, true," Riley said. "But that's *most* parents, right? I mean, give your mom some credit. She was listening to an indie-rock station on the car radio the other day."

"The tuner was broken. It was *stuck* on that station," Sierra explained.

Oh. Too bad, Riley thought. "Well, anyway, your mom's not so awful," she added. "I remember once she actually complimented my hair, and it was totally messy that day. It was back in my 'How many rubber bands can I use in one hairstyle?' phase. What I'm trying to say is, I'll bet you could make her understand why guitar is so important to you – if you'd try."

Sierra looked doubtful. "I'll think about it," she said as they headed back into the café and ordered two mochas. At the last minute Sierra ordered hers to go.

"You're not staying?" Riley was surprised.

"I've got band practice," she explained. "I didn't realise how late it was."

Oh. Too bad again, Riley thought. She checked out the Newsstand. The place was packed with people from West Malibu High, which was cool. But was this really how she wanted to spend her break? Just hanging around with the same people she saw every day of the school year?

"Make mine to go, too," she told Lennon, who was scrambling around behind the coffee bar.

"How come?" Sierra asked. "You're coming to band practice? I thought you and Alex were sort of over."

Alex Zimmer was the lead guitar player in The Wave. He and Riley had dated earlier in the year, but that had cooled down.

"No, I'm going to take a walk through town," Riley said. "It's such a beautiful day. I'm thinking, if I do something different, then maybe something different will happen to me."

"Okay. Call me later," Sierra said as the two of them parted at the door.

Riley sipped her mocha and walked through the crowded streets of Malibu. The weather was perfect, and everyone seemed to be in a good mood. Cars cruised through town and every single convertible top was down.

Now *there's* a cool car, Riley thought, spotting a vintage red Mercedes sports car with white leather seats. Then she realised that the man behind the wheel looked familiar.

Wait a minute, Riley thought. That's him! That's Jacques D'Oisseau!

No wonder Mom and Manuelo were so psyched about him, she realised. In person, the man radiated glamour. He had a white scarf thrown around his neck, which made his wavy silver hair look cool, somehow, instead of just ancient.

How come he's driving so slowly? she wondered.

Jacques had the top down on the Mercedes, and an adorable little fuzzy white poodle hung over the edge of the passenger-side door. The car was going so slowly Riley could walk faster than he drove. He kept craning his neck, looking around as if he were lost or something.

He spotted Riley staring at him. "Hello! Pardon me," he said in his totally charming French accent. He pulled the car to the curb. "Do you know where Dr. Mandleson's office is?"

"The vet?" Riley nodded. "Sure."

Of course she knew where Dr. Mandleson's office was. She and Chloe had been there a bunch of times right after they got their new cocker spaniel, Pepper.

"It's sort of hard to find," Riley explained. "But it's just two blocks away. Go down that street, turn right behind the muffin shop, and you're there." She pointed. "You can park around the back."

Jacques tossed up his hands and looked at her pleadingly. "I've been around the block three times!" he said. "And I didn't see it. Could you possibly show me?"

"Sure," Riley said as Jacques hopped out of the car with his puppy. They started walking. "You're Jacques D'Oisseau, aren't you?"

Jacques smiled. "I'm surprised someone your age recognised me," he said, bowing slightly in her direction.

"Oh, I didn't," Riley blurted out. "I mean, I probably wouldn't have recognised you, but my mom showed me your picture. She said you rented a house near us. I'm Riley Carlson."

Jacques laughed, and Riley instantly blushed.

"I am charmed to make your acquaintance, Miss Carlson," Jacques said, smiling and shaking her hand awkwardly across the armful of puppy he was carrying. "Which house is yours?"

"The boxy white one with a lot of glass and a deck facing the water," Riley said.

"That sounds like half the houses on the beach," Jacques replied with a laugh.

Yeah, I guess it does, Riley thought, blushing more. What is it about movie stars that makes you go all tongue-tied?

"Well, I'm sure I will see you on the beach," Jacques said. "And then you can point out your house to me."

"Okay," Riley said as they reached the end of the street. "Here we are." Riley turned into the alley by the muffin shop. "Dr. Mandleson's office is up those stairs."

"Ah!" Jacques said, as if he never would have found it without her. "*Merci*. You have saved my life."

"No problem," Riley said as Jacques headed towards the office.

"See you back home on the beach!" Jacques called before he climbed the stairs. "*Au revoir!*"

"*Au revoir*," Riley called back, grinning to herself. How cool, she thought. I just said good-bye in French! Then she turned to head back up the street – and smacked right into a guy standing behind her. "Oh! Excuse me!" Riley gasped. Then she gasped again when she saw who it was.

Not just any guy. He was tall, almost six feet, and blond and buff. His pale blue T-shirt fit snugly over his muscular chest. It matched his intense, ocean-blue eyes, which were rimmed with dark lashes. And he had dimples so deep, they made him look as if he was always smiling.

Riley's heart raced. Not just because he was cute, but because she recognised *him*, too.

I don't believe it, she thought. That's Marc Hudson! The son of the famous actor Richard Hudson.

11

What is this? Two-for-the-price-of-one celebrity day?

"Hi," Marc said, giving her a totally flirty smile. He stood there staring, as if he knew her or something. As if he thought they should talk.

"Uh, hi," Riley said. Please don't say something stupid! she warned herself.

"You're the third person I've actually *bumped into* today. I always heard Malibu was a small town, but this is ridiculous," he joked.

"Oh, it's a small town," Riley said, "but there's room for one more."

[**Riley: Hey. A little cheese never hurt anyone, right?**]

Marc smiled. "Wow, I never thought I'd run into someone like you on my first day here."

Someone like me? Riley's heart did a double thud. "This is your first day in Malibu?" she asked, trying to sound calm even though she wanted to scream, "Hey, everybody! Look! I'm flirting with Marc Hudson!!!"

He nodded. "Winter break. I live in New York, but I'm visiting my dad for the week." He glanced at his watch. "Actually, I've got to go, 'cause he's waiting for me."

"Oh." Riley said. She tried not to let her disappointment show.

"Yeah, he needs to lay a major shopping trip on me," Marc went on. "You know, buying me stuff to make up for the fact that we don't live together twenty-four/seven."

"Yeah, you don't want to miss *that*," Riley said.

"Oh, I don't really care about the stuff," he said. "But you've got to take pity on the guy, you know? It would hurt his feelings if I didn't do the bonding thing with him. Anyway, do you want to have coffee with me on Monday?"

Day after tomorrow? Riley was totally psyched. "Sure," she said. "Where?"

"Starbucks on Pearl Street?" He started walking away. "Meet me at two."

"Okay," Riley called. "But wait! You don't even know my name!"

"Oh, I know who you are," Marc said as he climbed onto a seafoam green motorbike that was parked near the curb. "You're Jacques D'Oisseau's daughter, Danielle. By the way, your English is really good!" He started up the engine and put on his helmet.

Wait! Riley wanted to say. That's wrong. I'm *not* Jacques D'Oisseau's daughter! But it was too late. Marc was pulling away.

Besides, she had always wanted to meet Marc Hudson.

And those eyes! How could she resist those eyes?

"A*u revoir*," she called after him with a guilty wave.

chapter two

"**L**ennon, name three things you want to do over winter break," Chloe said as she leaned against the counter in the Newsstand. She was hanging out with her boyfriend while he was at work.

"Huh?" Lennon ladled foam onto a cappuccino without looking up.

"And don't say 'make a mocha, a cappuccino and a half-caff latte,'" Chloe joked. "I mean, three *fun* things. Like, we could make a fire on the beach, bring a CD player and listen to nothing but songs with *fire* in the title," Chloe suggested. "Number Two: we could rent a motorbike, and you could teach me how to ride it. And Number Three..."

Her voice trailed off. He's not listening, Chloe thought, staring at his thick brown hair. He's totally wrapped up in making that coffee, and then the next one, and then the next...

"Sorry," Lennon said, glancing up and shooting

her a smile. "I've got to do four more of these and then we can talk, okay?"

"Okay," Chloe agreed. "I have something to ask you." She had been waiting for the right moment to ask if he knew anything about the commercial Jacques D'Oisseau was shooting at the Newsstand. But she knew the right moment was *not* while he was making coffees.

Meanwhile, I'll just stand here for the rest of my life, watching him make lattes, Chloe thought. Not that he didn't look adorable doing it!

"Hi, Chloe," Mr. Horner said, passing her on his way to the back room. "You here *again*? Maybe I should put you on the payroll."

Mr. Horner was the manager of the Newsstand. He was a Type-A bald guy with more energy than a birthday party full of sugared-up three-year-olds. He was getting used to seeing Chloe hanging around all the time.

"Maybe you should!" Chloe joked back. At least that way I'd get to hang out with Lennon once in a while, she thought.

When Lennon finished making the four coffees, he started cleaning the espresso machine.

"Lennon, do you think you'll have any time off this week?" Chloe asked, trying not to sound naggy or anything. "Because I don't know whether you've noticed, but I'm spending as much time with Mr. Horner as I am with you."

"I know, I know. I'm sorry," Lennon said. "You've been here so much, I'll bet you know my job almost as well as I do."

"Better," Chloe replied.

"Hey, don't push it," Lennon teased. "You *know* I'm the Latte-Meister."

"Test me!" Chloe demanded, enjoying the chance to have a conversation with him, even if it *was* about making coffee.

"Okay." Lennon glanced up as he emptied espresso grounds into a trash can. "Tell me, how much is a Tall Mochaccino?"

"Two ninety-five," Chloe said. "Three sixteen with tax."

"Very good." Lennon nodded.

"Test me again," Chloe said, loving the challenge.

"Can't," Lennon said. "I've got to go in the back and get some milk and then make two more lattes for the Randersons, who just walked in the door. They never even order any more. They just shoot me a look that says, 'Here we are. Serve us.'"

"Want me to make them?" Chloe offered. After all, she thought, it would be better than standing around doing nothing.

"I wish," Lennon said. "Wouldn't it be cool if you could get a job here? Then we could hang out all the time."

Chloe slapped her hand on the counter in excitement. "Why not?" she said. "That would be perfect!"

I could use the money, Chloe thought. And a job working with Lennon would be awesome! Besides, if I'm working here, maybe I'll have a chance to watch Jacques D'Oisseau film his commercial!

"Are you serious?" Lennon's face lit up.

"Definitely," Chloe said. She glanced around for the manager. "Mr. Horner just *said* he should put me on the payroll. Maybe he wasn't joking. I'll go ask him."

Lennon held up a finger. "No, wait. His moods can be tricky. Let me ask him when he's not so busy. We've got to time this right."

Fine with me, Chloe thought. And anyway, two of her best friends, Tara and Quinn, had walked in ten minutes ago, and she wanted to talk to them. Chloe wandered over to their table and sat down.

"Hi," Tara said, sounding as bored as Chloe felt.

"Hi," Chloe said. She reached over and stole a piece of the muffin Quinn was eating. "What's up? Anything good?"

"Nada, zero, zilch," Tara said, shaking her head. "You know what the problem with living in Malibu is? When it's time for break, everyone else in the country heads for the beach to kick back and party like it's 1999. But we already *live* at the beach!"

"I know," Chloe said. "What are we supposed to do? Take a road trip to Canada to go curling or something?"

"What's curling?" Quinn frowned, puzzled.

"You don't want to know," Tara answered. "It's like

17

shuffleboard on ice with a broom. Believe me, you've got to be seriously desperate for entertainment to even consider it."

"Actually, I think I've got my winter break plans lined up," Chloe said.

"Can I come?" Quinn asked quickly.

Chloe shook her head. "I'm not going anywhere. I'm staying right here and working with Lennon."

"As a coffee waitress?" Tara looked only mildly impressed. "Hey, whatever floats your boat."

"No, really, it's an excellent plan," Chloe explained. "For one thing, I'll get to hang out with him constantly. What could be better? Besides, something cool is going to happen here."

"Tell," Tara said.

Chloe leaned forward and lowered her voice. "Have you ever heard of Jacques D'Oisseau?" she asked.

Tara looked blank, but Quinn nodded.

"French actor," Quinn explained to Tara. "My mom is obsessed with him. He was in some famous classic movie called *Tunnel of Rain*. I think he directed it, too. My mom thinks he's a total hottie."

"Right. Well, he rented a house near us and he's going to direct a coffee commercial for the Super Bowl," Chloe explained in a whisper. "And they're shooting it right here at the Newsstand next Saturday. So I'm hoping I can watch them during the filming."

"Seriously? Now *that* would be way cool," Tara

admitted. "In fact, you should totally audition for a part!"

"Oh, no way," Chloe said. "I've heard the set is going to be closed."

"So what?" Tara urged her. "You'll already be *inside*, working here! With your charm, you could talk this Jacques guy into an audition for sure!"

"Have you met him yet?" Quinn asked. "My mom will be so jealous."

Chloe started to shake her head, but just then Lennon hurried over.

"Okay, you've got the job," he said, looking happy and wiping his hands on his apron. "Mr. Horner said you can start on Monday."

"Cool!" Chloe jumped up and threw her arms around Lennon's neck. "Thank you, thank you!"

Lennon wrapped his arms around her waist and squeezed. "Hey, don't thank me," he whispered into her ear. "It's going to be awesome seeing you all the time."

Chloe beamed. She couldn't believe she was going to get *paid* to hang out with her honey! And with any luck, she might even get a part in a Superbowl commercial! Tara was right. She could probably charm her way into an audition at least.

It looked as if winter break wasn't going to be so boring after all!

chapter
three

"Chloe, what if he only asked me out because he thought I was famous? Because he thought I was Danielle D'Oisseau?" Riley worried out loud the next morning.

She and Chloe were sitting out on the deck of their house, eating a breakfast of yogurt and fruit.

"No way," Chloe said. "For one thing, I've never heard of her, so you're not *that* famous."

"I'm famous enough!" Riley argued. "My dad's a major French movie star!"

"*Your* dad lives in a trailer down the beach," Chloe reminded her.

[Riley: Oops. Right. Ever since our parents separated, Dad's been living the life of a beach bum. You know, relaxing, doing his own thing. He used to run a fashion business with our mom, but he decided it wasn't for him.]

"But that's only because he's trying to find himself, or something," Riley said. "You know Dad. He's searching for his inner granola. He *could* live in a house like ours if he wanted to."

Chloe nodded. "My point is, Jacques D'Oisseau is *not* your dad, and you've got to tell Marc Hudson the truth."

"Absolutely," Riley said firmly. "Except, what if…I mean, if he…"

"Don't stress," Chloe said. "I'm sure he asked you out because he thought you were cute. Not just because you're Jacques D'Oisseau's daughter."

"Yeah," Riley agreed, glancing at her reflection in the sliding glass doors that led to the deck.

[<u>Riley</u>: Okay, so I have bed-head right now, my eyes are kind of puffy, and my pink pyjama top doesn't exactly match my red-and-blue-checked pyjama bottoms. But I'm going to do laundry today–I swear! By the time I see Marc tomorrow, I'll have it together.]

"It is weird, though," Chloe said as she popped a piece of pineapple into her mouth. "I mean, what made him think you were Danielle D'Oisseau?"

"Maybe I look like her," Riley said. "Wouldn't that be cool?"

"Not likely," Chloe said. "Jacques is tall and very European-looking, right?"

"True," Riley admitted. Riley and Chloe both had

21

blonde hair, big eyes, perfect teeth, and full lips. They looked as if they should have *Grown in California* stamped on their cheeks.

"So why *did* Marc think you were Jacques's daughter?" Chloe asked.

"I don't know," Riley said. "He probably heard me saying good-bye to Jacques."

"By the way, have you seen Jacques since then?" Chloe asked. "Because I have the most amazing idea. I'm thinking of asking him for an audition for his commercial!"

"Seriously?" Riley's eyes lit up.

Chloe nodded. "It was Tara's idea. She said since I'll be working at the Newsstand already, I should give it a shot. I was hoping maybe you could introduce me to Jacques, though."

"I haven't seen him since we met on the street," Riley said. Then she was quiet for a moment. "I wonder what she looks like."

"Who?" Chloe asked.

"Danielle," Riley said. "I mean, I wonder if I could possibly pass for her."

"You don't *want* to, do you?" Chloe asked.

Riley shrugged. "I don't know. I'm just curious."

"Well, there's one way to find out!" Chloe said, jumping up. "Come on."

A minute later the two of them were huddled over Chloe's computer in their bedroom. Chloe logged on to the Internet and did a search on Danielle

D'Oisseau's name. A zillion Websites came up, but they were all about Jacques.

"It says here that Jacques' kids grew up in Europe, but they were kept out of the limelight," Chloe reported. "I can't find a single site with a picture of his kids."

"How old are they now?" Riley wondered aloud.

Chloe clicked down the screen to a biography section. "Danielle is fourteen," she reported. "And she has a half brother who's twenty."

"She's my age!" Riley said brightly.

"Down, girl," Chloe said. She clicked on to another window. "It says here that Danielle was born during a brief marriage between Jacques D'Oisseau and Faye Huntington."

Faye Huntington? Everyone knew who she was: a superfamous American actress who had dark hair and emerald-coloured eyes. Her trademark was a beauty mark on her cheek, and she always wore her hair swept up in a French twist.

Riley grabbed her hair and pushed it up behind her head. "What do you think? Do I look like her?"

"No!" Chloe said. "Don't even go there!"

"Yeah. I guess it *is* pretty lame," Riley admitted. She let her hair fall back down. "I'm just nervous about this date. It's going to be so hard to say, 'Hi, Marc. I realise you're the son of a gorgeous, famous movie star, but I'm just plain old Riley Carlson.'"

"Maybe you should throw in *poor little* plain old

23

Riley Carlson. You know, really *sell* yourself," Chloe teased.

Riley would have laughed, but she was busy right then. She picked up an eyebrow pencil and used it to make a small beauty mark on her cheek.

"I told you, don't go there!" Chloe said when she saw what Riley was doing. "Stick to the truth!"

"Right," Riley said, dropping the pencil. After all, that's what she'd been telling Sierra to do.

I guess I'd better take my own advice! Riley decided. She rubbed off the beauty mark, changed into a pair of cute blue Capri pants and a small white camisole, and called Sierra.

"You want to hang out?" Riley asked.

"Definitely," Sierra said. "I'll come over."

Half an hour later Sierra arrived in a pair of preppy khaki slacks and a pink polo shirt. It took her under two minutes to change into low-rise black jeans and a royal blue tank top.

Then Riley grabbed the dog's leash and they took the Carlsons's brown and white cocker spaniel, Pepper, for a walk on the beach.

For the first ten minutes Riley grilled Sierra for ideas about what to wear on her date with Marc tomorrow. Sierra thought black leather pants would make a sophisticated statement, but Riley pointed out that the weather was too warm for leather.

"I'd be sweating like a pig," Riley said. "And then

24

the leather would stick to my thighs and…forget it. The whole thing is too ugly to discuss."

They finally settled on Riley's cream sweater and brown jeans.

"So did you tell your parents about your band?" Riley asked as they trudged through the sand.

"Are you kidding?" Sierra shot Riley a look.

"No," Riley said. "I thought you were going to consider coming clean with them."

"Well, I did, and I decided against it," Sierra replied. "My parents are hopeless. They wouldn't get it. Listen, guess who just wrote a new song? Marta! Can you believe it?"

Marta was the keyboard player in Sierra's band, but she missed a lot of rehearsals. Riley got the feeling Marta didn't take The Wave as seriously as the rest of its members did.

"Really? Is it any good?" Riley asked.

"It's fabulous!" Sierra said. "It's called 'Random Access Misery.' The lyrics are amazing and the melody is awesome. There's only one problem."

"She wants to sing it?" Riley guessed.

Sierra nodded.

The two of them burst out laughing.

"She really can't hear herself!" Sierra said, jumping to avoid Pepper, who was getting tangled up in the leash. "She thinks she's on key, and no one wants to tell her she's not."

"Well, duh," Riley said. "I wouldn't want to be the

25

one to say, 'Oh, by the way, you sound like a porpoise with laryngitis when you sing.'"

[Riley: Now before you jump all over me for being so heartless about Marta's voice, let me clear up one thing. Those are not my words. I'm just quoting what Mrs. Henry, our third-grade teacher, used to say when Marta sang "The Star- Spangled Banner." Me, personally? I thought Marta sounded more like a Chihuahua choking on a dog biscuit.]

"And it's weird, because she's a great keyboard player," Sierra went on. "It's not as if she isn't musical or anything."

"So what are you going to do?" Riley asked.

Sierra started to answer, but just then Pepper pulled away, making Riley drop the leash.

"Pepper!" Riley called. "Hold on!" She ran to catch up with her dog, but Pepper was already racing towards a fluffy white puppy on the deck of a nearby house. The puppy was on a leash, but the leash was loosely looped over a post.

Hey, Riley thought as she ran to catch Pepper. That's Jacques D'Oisseau's house! The house her mother said he'd rented.

Then she recognised the dog – the same cute little white fuzzball Jacques had taken to the vet.

All at once the puppy got loose and ran down the steps to the beach. It scurried across the sand, romping and playing with Pepper, who began chasing it.

"Pepper! Stay!" Riley called, running and finally catching up with the dogs.

She took Pepper's leash and handed it to Sierra, who was standing nearby. Then she grabbed the poodle's leash and scooped the little dog up into her arms.

"This is Jacques D'Oisseau's dog," Riley explained to Sierra. "Wait here," she said, hurrying to return the poodle. "I'll be right back." She ran up the steps of Jacques' house and knocked on the sliding glass door.

A moment later he appeared and slid it open. "Ooh-la-la, she got away again?" He reached for the poodle. "Chaudette, you bad dog! Thank you for bringing her back," he said, looking up. "Oh! It's you! Hello again, Riley Carlson. You keep rescuing me and my dog!" Jacques reached out to shake Riley's hand.

"No problem," Riley said. "She's so cute. What's her name again?"

"Chaudette," Jacques said, pronouncing it like *show-dett*. "It means little bundle of warmth." He smiled and hugged the dog.

Riley could see why he was a big movie star. His smile lit up his whole face.

"Well, thank you again for bringing her back," Jacques said. "If you see her get loose again, please just open this glass door and put her inside. This door is like your 7-Eleven stores – always open."

"Okay," Riley said, laughing. "I will."

Jacques closed the door, and Riley hurried back to Sierra. Wow, she thought. He's so nice! Wouldn't it be cool if I *were* part of his life?

For half a second she thought again about pretending to be Jacques' daughter in front of Marc Hudson. Why not? It would be for one lousy date. Or two. Marc was only in Malibu for the winter break. He'd be going back to New York at the end of the week, right? He'd never have to know the truth.

[Riley: Okay, so that was a weak moment. What can I say? Besides, you shouldn't judge me until you've walked in my shoes. And by the way, they're size 6$\frac{1}{2}$. So if you find a cute pair that goes with these jeans, call me, okay?]

Who am I kidding? Riley thought. I just got done lecturing Sierra about leading a double life. So I definitely can't start doing it myself! She had to tell Marc the truth.

And if he doesn't like me anymore and never asks me out again? she thought, trying to prepare for the worst. I'll deal.

But in her heart she was really hoping that wouldn't happen.

chapter
four

"**W**ow," Lennon said, eyeing Chloe the next day at the Newsstand. "You look awesome in that Newsstand T-shirt."

"Really?" Chloe ducked, to try to catch her reflection in the glass of the pastry case.

"But then, you look great in everything you wear," Lennon added. "Except cinnamon. Come here. You got some on your nose." He reached up and brushed it off for her.

Chloe beamed and pulled back her hair, twisting it into a knot on top of her head. This is so awesome! she thought. I can't believe we're allowed to spend the whole day together – and I don't even have to apologise to Mr. Horner!

"I filled the cinnamon container and the milk and creamer things," Chloe said.

"I can see that," Lennon said, staring at a big splotch of milk on her black apron. "Who knew you were such a klutz?"

"I'm *not* a klutz!" Chloe smiled. She loved the way he was making fun of her because she knew he didn't really mean it. "That milk container is heavy, that's all. Anyway, what do I do next, boss?"

"Next I teach you how to make espresso," Lennon said, taking her by the hand and leading her to the machine.

Chloe's heart skipped a beat when he touched her hand. They had been going out for six weeks, but she still got a rush whenever his arm brushed hers.

Cammie, a short girl with curly brown hair who also worked at the Newsstand, was busy making espresso for two customers. Lennon and Chloe stood watching, waiting their turn at the machine.

"Can I ask you something?" Chloe said as they waited.

"What?" Lennon asked.

"You know about the coffee commercial Jacques D'Oisseau is shooting, right?" Chloe asked. "Well, Tara said maybe I should try to audition for a part."

"Yeah, you should ask him," Lennon agreed. "I hear the auditions are on Thursday."

Thursday? Today was Monday, so the auditions were only a few days away.

"He comes in here every morning at around nine," Lennon added.

Chloe shot a glance at the clock. Too bad she was working the afternoon shift. She'd have to be sure to get to work early tomorrow.

"Lennon?" Mr. Horner called from the back. He gestured towards some messy tables in the café. "Could you tear yourself away long enough to clean up tables three and four?"

"Oh. Sorry," Lennon said, dashing off. "Uh, Cammie can show you how to make espresso," he called to Chloe.

Chloe's heart sank. It would be more fun if *he* could teach me, she thought.

Cammie ran through the instructions quickly, explaining what went into each kind of drink. "The whole thing's pretty easy and obvious," she said when they were done. "So I'll take the orders, and you can make the hot beverages."

Whoa. Just like that? Don't I get to practise for a few days or something?

Nope. Guess not, Chloe realised when Cammie called out the first three orders.

"Regular coffee, tall cappuccino, and a grande mocha, but light on the chocolate," Cammie said.

Chloe made all three drinks and set them on a tray. She carried them out to table seven, where the customers were waiting.

"Hey, Peaches," Lennon said, calling Chloe by a nickname he had started using. "Nice job serving those drinks."

[<u>Chloe</u>: Wait! Before you get the wrong idea, let me explain. I mean, seriously. Peaches? The thing is, Lennon has a cousin called Peaches, and we were talking about it last week – about how we both think it's, like, the corniest nickname in the world. So then he started calling me Peaches, just to be funny. And I laughed every time. So of course he kept it up.]

"Thanks, Sugar-face," Chloe said, joking back.

[<u>Chloe</u>: That's the other part of the routine. He calls me Peaches, and then I come back with some really icky pet name for him. But I use a different one each time.]

"Gag me," Lennon said.

Chloe laughed. "I win!" she announced, happy.

"Excuse me," the man at table seven said, interrupting them. "But you put chocolate in my coffee."

"And there's no chocolate in this mocha," the woman with him added.

Uh-oh. Chloe felt her stomach tighten. How did I mess up *that*? she wondered.

"What's the problem here?" Mr. Horner asked, appearing from behind the counter.

"Our drinks are all wrong," the man at the table said.

Mr. Horner scowled at Chloe. "This job isn't so hard," he said to her. "You simply have to make coffee, and make it right. That's all I ask."

"Sorry," Chloe apologised, feeling her face turning red.

"Don't worry, Mr. Horner." Lennon scooped up the drinks. "I'll fix it pronto. Don't hold this against Chloe. It's only her first day."

"I won't hold it against her," Mr. Horner said briskly. "I'll hold it against you. *You* recommended her."

Lennon hurried back to the counter and Chloe followed him.

"Thanks, Lennon," she said softly.

"No problem, Peaches," he whispered, giving her a smile. "Just try not to goof up again. It's the one thing Mr. Horner gets cranky about. You've got to concentrate when you're making the drinks."

Chloe nodded. "Don't worry. I will."

"Did you get those last two?" Cammie called from the register.

"Huh?" Chloe glanced over and realised there was a long line of people waiting to be served. "Uh, no. Can you repeat them?"

Cammie sighed and called out the orders again, and Chloe got to work.

Who knew your hands would get so tired from squeezing this espresso thing over and over? Chloe thought after she'd made about seven of them. She glanced at the clock. It was only one-fifty. She hadn't even been there an hour.

"Chloe! Hi!" a voice called from a few feet in front of the counter. "What are you doing back *there*?"

Chloe glanced up just as she was putting a double latte onto the counter for a customer. "Amanda! Hi!" she called back, seeing her friend Amanda Gray.

Just then the double latte tipped off the counter – towards the customer who was waiting for it. It splattered all over the floor.

"Whoa!" the woman cried out. She was wearing an expensive-looking business suit and heels, but she managed to jump back just in time.

Oh, no! Chloe raced out from behind the counter to clean up the mess. "Did it spill on you?" she asked the woman.

"Almost." The woman brushed at her skirt. "I felt a few drops splash my legs, but I guess I'm all right."

This is a nightmare! Chloe thought. I can't seem to do anything right!

Lennon rushed over and started helping Chloe clean up, mopping the spill with paper towels. "Don't worry. Everyone drops one the first week they work here," he said.

He's being so nice! Chloe thought. She glanced up and saw Amanda watching her with a worried look on her face.

Amanda was another one of Chloe's good friends from school. She had been very quiet and shy when Chloe first met her, but lately she'd begun to come out of her shell.

She waited until Chloe finished cleaning up and

was making a new double latte for the woman. Then she came up to the counter.

"Whoa. Rough day," Amanda said. "I didn't even know you were working here."

"I just started," Chloe explained. Then she lowered her voice. "I thought it was going to be great being near Lennon all day. And it is. But I didn't think working at a coffee house would be so hard."

Amanda nodded. "Tell me about it."

"You want something?" Chloe asked. "I'll be your friend forever if you don't order anything hot."

Amanda laughed. "Okay, give me an iced chai," she said.

"Thank you!" Chloe said, getting to work.

By the time she brought the chai to Amanda, the café had cleared out. So Chloe sat to talk for a minute. "Did you hear about Riley?" she asked, leaning in to share the great news. "She ran into Marc Hudson – you know, Richard Hudson's son – and he asked her out! She's probably with him right now."

"That's cool," Amanda said with a shrug.

That's typical of Amanda, Chloe thought. She wasn't impressed just because someone was a celebrity. That's what Chloe liked about her. Amanda was so real and down to earth.

"And the other really amazing news is that they're shooting a commercial here at the Newsstand on Saturday," Chloe went on. "I'm hoping I can worm my way into it. Lennon says the auditions are on Thursday."

"How about auditioning for the part of coffee waitress right *now*?" came a grouchy voice from behind Chloe.

Chloe whirled around and saw Mr. Horner standing there with his hands on his hips. She jumped up. "Oh, sorry," she said, hurrying back to work. I guess there are *two* things that make him cranky! she thought.

For the next few hours Chloe tried to get the orders right. And she tried not to spill on anyone. And she tried not to spend too much time talking to Amanda, Tara and Quinn, who all came into the Newsstand.

But it was hard – especially the last one. Her friends kept talking to her every time she brought a coffee out to one of the other customers.

By the end of the day Chloe was so tired, she just wanted to lie down in a hot tub and never get up. Maybe this was a mistake, she thought. Maybe working at the Newsstand *wasn't* the best possible way to spend winter break.

"Hey, Peaches," Lennon said as they were closing up that night. "You want to catch a movie?"

Chloe looked at him as if he were nuts. "I'm wiped. I'm going straight home to bed."

"Wow," Lennon said. "You *are* tired. You didn't even call me a sickening nickname."

Chloe didn't answer. She was too tired to think of a snappy comeback, too tired to even speak!

"Okay, well, I'll see you tomorrow morning," Lennon said. "Mr. Horner wants you on the early shift this time, so we'll open up together. Be here at six."

Six in the morning? Chloe's eyes popped open. Was he kidding? She stared at Lennon, waiting for him to laugh.

But he was serious.

chapter
five

Riley checked her reflection in the glass door before she entered Starbucks.

I've got to look good, she thought nervously. Majorly good. Good enough to make up for the fact that I'm not French, not famous, and not the daughter of Jacques D'Oisseau.

In her low-rise brown jeans and cream sweater, Riley thought she'd probably pulled it off. The outfit was totally cute and her hair had been in a good mood that morning. It fell perfectly around her face.

"Hi there," Marc said, standing up the moment he saw her.

Good manners! Riley loved that.

Marc was wearing a white T-shirt under an unbuttoned black cotton shirt. And black jeans. Plus he wore a small woven leather necklace with a turquoise bead on it – just like the one Riley was wearing.

"Hi," Riley said, tilting her head so that her hair swung back and forth a little.

"Great necklace," Marc said, shooting her a smile the instant he noticed it.

"Thanks," Riley said with a grin. "It's my fave because no one else has one like it."

Marc laughed and picked up the cup of coffee on the table. "I got here early," he explained. "Needed a double espresso big-time. What can I get you?"

"Just a regular coffee," Riley said.

Marc went to the counter and got her coffee. Then he sat down, leaned forward, and said, "Okay, tell me everything about you."

[Riley: **Everything about me? You mean, like starting with the fact that my name is really Riley Carlson, not Danielle D'Oisseau? And that I'm totally lying about who I am?**]

Riley tried to think of how to word it, but her throat closed up and her mind went blank. "No, you go first," she said finally.

Marc nodded. "Okay."

Quickly he told her that he was an only child. That he'd grown up in New York City. That he was now a junior at a private school there. And that he loved movies. "Besides that, I love the beach."

"I do, too!" Riley said.

"And hip-hop music, especially Master Crush," Marc went on. "And I'm a total zombie in the morning. And that's everything you need to know about me."

"That's incredible," Riley said.

"How come?" Marc asked.

"Well, I *adore* the beach," Riley said. "And I'm a complete maniac about Master Crush. And I'm really cranky if I don't get enough sleep."

"Wow. It's as if you're my twin or something," Marc said, grinning.

Riley almost burst out laughing. You have no idea how funny that is! she thought. She had to bite her tongue to keep from saying, "I already have a twin! My sister, Chloe!"

"Okay, here's a question," Riley said. "If you could have gone anywhere for winter break, where would it be?"

"That's easy," Marc said, smiling. "Malibu."

"Really?" Riley felt her face glowing.

Marc nodded. "For one thing, Malibu has some amazing people." He grinned at her even more. "And my dad really wanted me to come out here. He's trying to get me to spend more time with him."

"That's nice," Riley said.

Wow. He's so easy to talk to, she thought. She was having such a great time, she hated to spoil the mood by saying, "Oh, by the way, I'm not who you think I am." But she had to tell him…soon.

"You want to go hang out at the beach?" Marc asked.

"Sure." Riley took one last sip of her coffee.

They headed to the beach, and as they walked past her house, Riley tried not to glance up at the deck. What if Manuelo sees me? she thought. He might call me by my real name. She turned her back to the house and strolled down to the water.

"Want to skip stones?" Marc asked. "I'm a pro."

"Hey, you're talking to a stone-skipping champ," Riley shot back. "You don't want to mess with me."

"Bring it on!" Marc bent down to pick up a pebble.

Riley found a thin flat rock. She turned sideways to the water and flicked her stone. It skipped across the waves in three perfect arcs.

Marc stared for a minute. "Okay. That was good," he admitted. He cleared his throat and walked a few steps. Then he bent his knees and flicked his wrist, sending the rock skipping. It went farther than Riley's, but it only skipped twice.

"I'd give that an eight," Riley teased him.

"No way!" Marc complained. "That thing landed in Japan!"

They both laughed and continued walking down the beach.

"So anyway, Danielle, what's the deal with the commercial your dad is shooting?" Marc asked. "Are you totally pumped about it?"

"Well, uh…" Riley sputtered. Tell him now, she thought. Just say it. He's *not* my dad. He's just the guy who rented a house down the beach from us.

41

But she was having so much fun, she didn't want to spoil the mood. Besides, Marc didn't wait for an answer. He kept rambling on about how much he loved Jacques' movie, *Tunnel of Rain*. How he had seen it shown as a classic re-release at the Cannes Film Festival in Nice last year. And how he was hoping to hang out at the commercial shoot later this week.

Riley glanced up. They were approaching Jacques' beach house.

"I am so into your dad's career," Marc said. "I mean, I've heard that this commercial he's directing is going to be really cool. People say it's going to be shot in black-and-white, right? Sort of like an old detective movie from the 1940s."

Riley swallowed hard and took a deep breath. "To tell you the truth, he's not my dad," she said.

Marc tilted his head. "Huh?"

"You made a mistake," Riley said. "My name is Riley Carlson, not Danielle D'Oisseau. I'm not Jacques' daughter."

"Are you serious?" Marc looked shocked. And maybe disappointed. Riley couldn't tell.

"Yeah," Riley said. "It was a mistake. I…" She was about to explain the whole thing to him. But as they neared the house, Jacques's little white poodle ran down the steps and onto the sand.

"Chaudette!" Riley called, running to catch the puppy. "Chaudette! Come back!"

The puppy stopped when she heard Riley shouting her name. Then she turned and raced to Riley.

"Sorry," Riley said to Marc. "Hang on a minute. I've got to put her inside."

Riley hurried up the steps of Jacques' house. Marc followed her as she opened the sliding glass door a few inches and put the puppy inside.

"Now you stay where you belong, understand?" Riley said. She closed the door and turned to see Marc standing beside her.

He gazed in through the glass door towards the fireplace mantel. Sitting right there, on top, was a Golden Globe award.

Marc smiled. "Don't tell me you're not Danielle D'Oisseau," he said. "That Golden Globe was for *Tunnel of Rain*, the film your parents starred in and your dad directed."

"They're not my parents!" Riley said. "Honestly! I'm just a girl from Malibu who lives down the beach."

Marc shook his head slowly, grinning the whole time. "You don't have to lie to me," he said. "I know what it's like being a famous person's kid. Once people find out, they try to use you, and it ruins everything. Believe me, I've been there."

Riley tried to interrupt him, but Marc didn't want to hear it. He was sure she was Danielle D'Oisseau.

"Don't worry, your secret is safe with me," he said. "People like us have to stick together. That's why I only hang out with people connected to show business. Other people just don't understand."

What? Riley froze. He only hangs out with people connected to show business? Does that mean he'd dump me if I made him face the truth?

For half a second Riley was going to blurt it all out anyway. How he had mistaken her for Danielle D'Oisseau when she was leading Jacques to the vet.

But she couldn't do it. Not if it meant Marc would walk away. They were having so much fun together! She didn't want it to end. Maybe if he got to know her, he'd start to like her for herself. She could always tell him the truth later, right?

"Yeah, okay," Riley said with a shrug. "But don't tell anyone who I am. I'm trying to keep a low profile."

"No problem." Marc nodded. "I'm all about keeping a low profile myself. So do you want to go out again?"

Huh? Is this date over? Riley wondered. Then she realised he thought he'd dropped her off at home! He was ready to be on his way.

"Uh, sure!" Riley said.

"How about catching *Les Enfants Verts* at the Pepperdine campus Wednesday night? I saw a sign posted in town. It's open to the public, and it's supposed to be a really funny film," he said. "Unless you've already seen it."

It's obviously a French film, Riley said to herself. And judging from the way Marc said the title – with a perfect French accent – he must speak French really well.

"I haven't seen it yet," Riley said. "It sounds great."

"Excellent," Marc said. "They're showing it without subtitles, which will be awesome. I hate how the subtitles get in the way, don't you?"

No subtitles? Yikes! You mean I've got to sit through an entire French movie without understanding more than three words?

"Yeah, great," Riley said, trying to sound enthusiastic instead of morose.

"So I'll meet you Wednesday night at seven," Marc said as he walked towards the deck steps.

"See you then," Riley called, still standing by Jacques' back door.

When Marc was gone, she headed towards her own house.

What have I got myself into? she wondered.

Well, at least she had a plan. She'd tell him the truth when he knew her better. When he liked her for herself.

But for now there was only one choice.

She had to pretend to be French!

chapter
six

"Chloe! I told you yesterday, no amaretto syrup in the hot-milk container!" Lennon said.

"Oh. Sorry!" Chloe shot Lennon a cute but guilty smile. "I forgot."

Lennon sighed and shook his head. "Well, it's your third day on the job," he grumbled. "Try to remember next time. I just made three lattes that tasted like almonds."

Uh-oh, Chloe thought. That was bad. Lennon *had* told her on her second day to be careful about the almond syrup because some people were allergic to nuts.

She gulped, feeling even more guilty. Still, she couldn't believe he was being so grumpy.

[<u>Chloe</u>: **Honestly, I have never seen Lennon in such a bad mood. Of course, I've never spent three whole days with him, either. Especially three days when I've made so**

[many dumb mistakes in a row. Yesterday was the worst. I accidentally spilled a huge bag of coffee beans all over the floor. Mr. Horner said it was a fifty-dollar loss. And Lennon took the blame, even though it was my fault. He was really nice about it, saying, "Don't worry, you'll learn. Those bags are heavy." But that was yesterday. Today he looks like he's ready to toss me into the coffee grinder!]

"What's the problem here?" Mr. Horner asked, looking over Lennon's shoulder.

"Oh, no problem," Lennon said quickly. "I've got everything under control."

"I hope so," Mr. Horner said. He glanced at Chloe and walked away.

Yikes! Chloe thought. Mr. Horner was breathing down their necks already, and it was only eight-thirty in the morning! She waited for the manager to slip into the back room. Then she whispered to Lennon. "Do you want me to apologise to the customers personally?"

"It might help," Lennon admitted. "Go out there and do damage control. I'll remake their drinks and put them up on the counter. When they're ready, you can serve them."

Good deal, Chloe thought. Damage control was something she could do! She wiped her hands on her apron, tossed her hair over her shoulders, and walked up to the group of three women who were waiting for their coffees. They looked like tourists.

"Listen, I'm really sorry about the coffees," she said. "It was totally my fault. But we're getting it fixed right now, okay? I'm new on the job," she added, hoping that would help.

"Fine," one of the women said briskly, as if she didn't want to be interrupted.

Chloe glanced back at the counter. Lennon still didn't have the new drinks ready. And Tara and Quinn had just walked in. "Hi!" she said, thrilled to see some friendly faces. "What's up?"

"Not much," Tara replied. "Except there's a huge sale at Smirmen's. All the bathing suits are fifty percent off. You want to come?"

"I can't," Chloe moaned. "I'm working another long shift."

"I *told* you this was a lousy way to spend the break," Tara said.

"So what happened with Riley's date the other day?" Quinn asked. "Did she and Marc Hudson hit it off?"

Hmm, Chloe thought. Maybe she shouldn't tell them that Riley was pretending to be French. Tara and Quinn were good friends, but they weren't so great at keeping secrets.

"They *totally* hit it off," Chloe said. "They're going out again tonight, I think. You guys want something to drink?"

"No, we just came in to talk," Tara admitted.

"And to find out if you're going to be in that commercial," Quinn said. "My mom was so jealous when I told her."

Chloe shrugged and leaned against one of the tables. "I don't have an audition lined up yet. Jacques came in yesterday morning at nine, but I was too nervous to talk to him. I ran and hid behind the pastry case!"

"No way!" Tara said. "Well, you've *got* to talk to him today. The auditions are tomorrow, right?"

Chloe nodded. "He should be here soon." She checked the clock. "He comes in every day at nine and orders coffee, a croissant and a copy of *Le Monde*."

"What's *Le Monde*?" Quinn asked.

"A French newspaper," Chloe replied.

Tara started to nod, but then she glanced at something behind Chloe's shoulder. "Oops. Maybe we'd better get going."

"Why?" Chloe whirled around and saw Lennon standing beside her with a scowl.

"Can we talk?" he said sharply. He didn't wait for an answer. He motioned for her to follow him into the back room.

"Uh, see you later," Chloe called to her friends as she followed Lennon.

"Look," Lennon said when they were alone. "You can't spend all morning talking to your friends. Those three coffees I made for the tourists were just sitting there on the counter, getting cold!"

49

"Oh, gosh, sorry!" Chloe covered her mouth. "I looked and I didn't think you had them ready yet."

Lennon gave her a seriously worried stare. "Listen, I know you're trying, but Mr. Horner is starting to lose patience. He took me aside a few minutes ago and basically laid it out."

"Laid what out?" Chloe asked.

"He said, 'You recommended her, so it's on your head if she messes up. Teach her how to do the job or fire her.'"

"Are you kidding?" Chloe gasped. "It's only my third day!"

Lennon's shoulders slumped. "I know, I know, but you can't make any more mistakes, okay?"

"I won't," Chloe promised.

But even if I do, you wouldn't really fire me, would you? she wanted to say, but she didn't.

He was her *boyfriend*, Chloe decided. No way would he fire her. Not when he knew how much she wanted to watch the commercial being filmed – and maybe get an audition with Jacques D'Oisseau.

Chloe headed out to the coffee bar and took an order. A few minutes later Jacques walked in. He ordered his usual, then sat down. Now's my chance! Chloe thought, glancing around and wondering where Mr. Horner was. Lennon and Mr. Horner had both disappeared.

Okay, Chloe thought as she made Jacques' coffee. I probably shouldn't leave the counter right now, but there are no other customers waiting. And this will only take a minute...

She slipped out from behind the counter and walked to Jacques' table. "Good morning," she said, setting the coffee down beside his newspaper. "Um, you're Monsieur D'Oisseau, aren't you?"

"*Oui*," he answered, not looking up from his paper.

"Um, well, may I ask you something?" Chloe said.

"Chloe!" Lennon called sharply from across the room. "What are you doing? We need you back here!"

Okay! Chloe thought. But can't it wait a second?

She couldn't believe Lennon was calling her right at that moment. He *knew* how important it was to her to talk to Jacques D'Oisseau.

And if I don't ask him for an audition right now, I'll never get the chance! she thought. The auditions are tomorrow!

She opened her mouth to speak to Jacques again, but Lennon had walked out from behind the counter. He shoved a rag into her hands. "Wipe up table six," he said, scowling. "Okay?"

Oh, all right, Chloe thought, trudging back to work.

What ever made me think working together was a good idea?

Riley sat in the middle seat of Mrs. Pomeroy's minivan, smiling to herself. She could hardly wait to see Marc again tonight. Even the fact that she had to sit through an entire French movie without subtitles didn't make her any less excited.

There was just something about him. He was so nice. And funny. And easy to talk to. She'd loved their first date together.

She hoped that he felt the same way and that he wouldn't change his mind when he found out she wasn't Jacques' daughter.

It's not easy leading a double life! Riley thought. I mean, I could probably do it for a while. It might even be fun to pretend to be French for a few days. But I would never want to fake being someone I'm not for months and months, the way Sierra has been.

"So drop us off on the Smirmen's side of the mall," Sierra told her mom. She was sitting next to her, in the front passenger seat.

"You aren't going to get another bathing suit, are you?" Mrs. Pomeroy asked. "I've already bought you three that you never wear."

"Three solid-coloured tank suits, Mom," Sierra complained. "They don't look good on me."

"They're not *all* solids," Mrs. Pomeroy said. "What about the navy blue and cream striped one?"

Sierra sighed and turned to look at Riley.

"Tell her." Riley mouthed the words silently so Mrs. Pomeroy wouldn't hear. She gestured at Sierra's mom, trying to get the point across to Sierra that it would be better to tell her mom the truth about her double life. About her music, and her name, and what she liked to wear. Then Sierra could be herself!

As it was, Sierra was sitting there in a navy blue polo shirt and pleated blue jeans. And she was going to have to be *seen* in that outfit as she walked into the mall! At least until she could get to a rest room to change.

"Just do it!" Riley whispered.

But Sierra shook her head and opened her eyes really wide. She was too scared.

Maybe she needs a little help, Riley thought. She reached into her backpack and pulled out a CD. It was a disk Sierra had just given her – a demo of her band.

On a whim – and before Sierra could stop her – Riley leaned forward in the van and popped the CD into the player.

"What's that?" Mrs. Pomeroy asked nicely as the pulsing rock music came on.

"That's Sierra's band!" Riley blurted out.

Sierra turned to glare at Riley.

Mrs. Pomeroy laughed. "Oh, right. I can hear the violin in the background," she said. "You have such a funny sense of humour, Riley."

Sierra hit the eject button on the CD player.

"Yeah, she's a regular hoot," Sierra said as they pulled up to the mall's front entrance.

"Have fun," Mrs. Pomeroy called as they jumped out of the van.

As soon as they were alone, Sierra grabbed Riley's wrist. "How could you do that?" she said. But she looked sort of excited – sort of pumped up – by the whole thing.

"Did you see your mom's face?" Riley said. "She didn't seem to hate the music. She was smiling!"

"I know, I know." Sierra was talking really fast. "That was kind of cool, wasn't it? But it was probably because she didn't believe it was me."

"Listen," Riley argued, "you'll never know unless you take a chance and tell her the truth."

"Oh, look who's talking!" Sierra said. "You haven't exactly been honest with Marc."

"You're right," Riley admitted. "But I'm going to change that – eventually."

They were walking through the mall entrance, but Sierra stopped in her tracks. "Okay," she said. "I'll make you a deal. I'll tell my mom the truth by the end of winter break if you'll come clean with Marc Hudson."

Riley thought about it. Yeah, that was fair. Besides, she was planning to tell Marc the truth sooner or later.

"Okay, deal," Riley said. And they slapped five, just like they used to when they were kids, to seal the agreement.

The mall was packed, so they didn't do much window-shopping. Too crowded. It was straight to Smirmen's, try on forty bathing suits, buy two, and then crash in the food court.

"Can you believe we've been here two hours and haven't run into anyone we know?" Sierra said. "That's got to be a record."

Riley nodded, but she wasn't surprised. A lot of people had left town for the week.

Sierra took the last bite of her hot, salty pretzel and wiped her fingers. "Well, I'm over this," she said. "Do you want to go hang out at my house till your big date?"

"Definitely. Besides, you said I could paw through your closet for something to wear tonight," Riley reminded her.

"Right," Sierra agreed, but she sounded doubtful. "Just remember, all my clothes – the ones you might actually *want* to wear – are wrinkled. They're smashed into a big box in the back of my closet where my mom won't see them."

"That's another reason you have to tell her the truth!" Riley urged. "If wrinkled ever goes out of style, you're in big trouble."

They took the bus home, grabbed some fruit for an afternoon snack, and started to head for Sierra's room. But just then Sierra's mom came in and began making conversation, quizzing them about their shopping trip.

"It was good," Riley answered. "I bought a bathing suit and so did Sierra."

"You did?" Sierra's mom glanced at her daughter, surprised.

Sierra shot Riley a glare that said, "Why did you tell?"

Riley leaned close to her friend and whispered, "What about our deal? I thought you were going to tell her the truth!"

For half a second Sierra and her mom glanced at each other. Mrs. Pomeroy seemed to be waiting for an explanation, and Sierra seemed to be trying to decide what to do next.

Riley reached into her backpack and pulled out the demo CD again. She handed it to Sierra, gesturing towards the CD player in the kitchen. "Go for it," Riley whispered.

Sierra hesitated, but finally she popped it into the machine. "Mom?" she said as the music came on. "Riley was telling the truth in the car. That's my band, The Wave. I play bass guitar."

Mrs. Pomeroy laughed nervously. As if she kind of thought it was a joke but wasn't sure.

"No, really, Mom," Sierra said. She popped the CD out and showed her the label. All the musicians were listed. It said, SIERRA ON BASS. "See? That's me."

"But your name is Sarah," her mother said, shaking her head.

"I know. That's what you and Dad call me," Sierra said, a little impatiently. "But I go by Sierra in the band."

"Your father and I call you Sarah because it's your name," Mrs. Pomeroy said. "Are you feeling all right, Sarah?"

"No, honestly, it's true!" Riley chimed in, trying to help. "And her band is awesome! You should go hear them sometime. They're playing this Friday night at the Voodoo Lounge."

"Whoa!" Sierra said, putting a sudden halt to the conversation.

Oops! Riley thought. Did I go too far?

Before Mrs. Pomeroy could say anything else, the phone rang. She went to answer it.

"Why did you tell her about the Voodoo Lounge?" Sierra whispered when her mother was gone.

"Why not?" Riley asked.

"I don't know." Sierra twisted her thick hair around her fingers. "It just sort of freaks me out. What if my parents come and they hate it? And they ground me forever or something?"

"Don't worry. It'll be fine. Trust me," Riley said.

She hoped she was right.

chapter
seven

"**B**onsoir. *Tu es très belle ce soir*," Marc said, speaking perfect French as he greeted Riley that night outside the auditorium. She had just arrived at the Pepperdine campus to meet him for the movie.

"Thank you," Riley said. But instantly her mind was spinning. What did he just say? I've only had a few months of French! she thought.

Okay, so maybe she did know some of those words. *Belle* meant beautiful. And *bonsoir* was good evening. She knew that much. But could she actually have a conversation in French? No way!

"*Ça va?*" Marc asked.

"Hey, let's not speak French," Riley said quickly. "I'm still working on my English, okay?"

Marc did a double take. "Are you kidding? You're still *working* on it? Wow, you're heavy-duty. I mean, how much more English do you need, anyway?"

"Oh, uh, I don't know," Riley stammered, trying to make up an excuse. "Maybe I'll try out for a part in a Shakespeare play someday."

"Oh." Marc shrugged. "Whatever. Anyway, we'd better go in. They're starting the film in five minutes."

Fine by me, Riley thought. He took her hand and squeezed it. It was nice walking into the darkened theatre with Marc.

But mostly she just wanted to get this part of the date over. After the movie, when they would probably go out for coffee – *that's* what she was looking forward to. Then she could start being herself again and talk about something other than French stuff.

They found two seats about halfway down in the auditorium. The place was only about a third full – mostly college students and professors, plus a few older people who were trying to look French, judging from all the long scarves they were wearing.

Riley sneaked a quick peek at Marc as the movie came on. He looked amazing in his grey knit shirt and black jeans.

He held her hand and sat back in his seat with a smile as the credits rolled. Then, almost immediately, he started laughing at the screen.

Uh-oh, Riley thought. This is a comedy, and I'm supposed to think it's funny, too.

From what Riley could tell, the movie was about this great-looking young woman with red hair who rode a motor scooter all over Paris. And some guy was trying to catch up with her. There was a scene with a lobster and another scene where a man from a butcher's shop chased them, screaming.

Basically, she couldn't follow it at all.

Marc glanced over at her with a little frown as if he wondered why she wasn't enjoying it.

Oops, Riley thought. Guess it's time to fake it! She forced a laugh, but it was a little late. Everyone else was quiet now.

The next time Marc laughed, Riley tried to laugh, too, but it sounded so bogus, he shot her another weird glance.

"You okay?" he whispered.

"Sure," Riley said, throwing in one of the few French words she was comfortable with. "*Oui.*"

Oh, man, Riley thought. Is this what Sierra goes through every day of her life? Pretending to be something she's not?

The next two hours were a lot of work. Riley tried to laugh when Marc laughed, and gasp when he gasped. Finally the film ended, and she jumped up, happy that her ordeal was over.

"So what did you think?" Marc asked.

"About what?" Riley said. Then it hit her. Duh! He wants to talk about the movie!

"You know what?" she said, thinking fast and talking even faster. "It might have seemed really funny to you, but to me – being French and everything – it was just way too obvious and clichéd."

Marc nodded. "Yeah, I kind of thought so, too," he said. "I mean, I went with it, because everyone else was laughing. But it really wasn't all that hilarious. So, do you want to go out for coffee?" he asked, taking her hand again as they walked.

"You bet," Riley said. At last the date could start for real!

Marc led the way to the spot where his motorbike was parked. He handed her a helmet, and they rode into town.

"Let's check out the Newsstand," Marc said, pulling over to the curb.

The Newsstand? Riley thought. Everyone in there knows me, and they know I'm *not* Danielle! They'll blow my cover for sure!

"Uh, that place gets so crowded," Riley said fast. "How about Starbucks instead?"

"Hey, crowds don't scare *me*," Marc said. "I'm a New Yorker, remember? Besides, I want to see this place where your dad is shooting the mega-commercial."

Oh, boy, Riley thought. This is going to be a disaster. But then she flashed back to that afternoon. She and Sierra hadn't run into anyone they knew at the mall. So maybe she'd get lucky. Maybe…

Marc opened the door to the Newsstand, and they stepped inside. Instantly Larry Slotnick spotted Riley from across the crowded café and rushed towards her.

Not now, Larry! Riley thought. Larry was her goofy next-door neighbour. He'd had a crush on her since they were little kids.

So much for luck. In about two seconds he was going to be close enough to call out her name. There was only one thing to do. "Larry!" she called, rushing forward to greet him before he could say a word. "You darling!"

Quickly she kissed Larry on both cheeks the way she'd seen everyone in the French movie do. Then she whispered into his ear, "Call me Danielle – not Riley. And pretend I'm French. Please! And I'll be your friend forever. I'll explain later."

"Whoa," Larry said, grinning at the cheek kissing. "What did I do to deserve this?"

"Larry, Marc. Marc, Larry," she said, introducing them to each other.

"Hi," Larry said. "You look great tonight, *Danielle*. Very *chic*." He said the last word with a heavy French accent.

Riley rolled her eyes. Don't lay it on too thick! she silently pleaded. "Thanks, Larry. Anyway, excuse us. We're going to sit alone and talk." She motioned towards a small table in a corner. Then she glanced around the Newsstand. Even though it was crowded, none of her friends were there.

Good, Riley thought. We'll have one quick coffee and then we'll go. Maybe I'll actually get away with this!

"What do you want to drink?" Marc asked, walking towards the counter.

"I'll have a cappuccino," Riley said.

Marc stopped and did a double take. "Seriously?"

"Uh, yeah," Riley said. "Is that a problem?"

"No, I'm just surprised." He shrugged. "I mean, I guess you've been in America so long, you're picking up odd habits."

Odd habits? Drinking cappuccino? Riley frowned. She didn't get it.

"Well, you grew up in France, right?" Marc said. "None of the Europeans I know drink cappuccino for anything other than breakfast."

They don't? Who knew? Riley thought, feeling a little silly. She tried to act as if she'd realised that all along. "You're right, I've picked up some pretty odd habits since I've been here," she mumbled, blushing. Such as lying about who I am! "Anyway, do you mind if I sit here while you get it? My feet are killing me."

Besides, Cammie's working the counter. And I don't want to have to kiss *her* on both cheeks to get her to not call me by my real name! Riley thought.

"No problem," Marc said.

Riley waited at the table while Marc ordered. Then he came back and sat down. "They're going to bring it out when it's ready," he said. He glanced around the café, looking impressed. "This place will make a great location for your dad's commercial. Have you seen the script?"

"Uh, no." Riley made a face. "I get tired of all that…" Her voice trailed off.

"All that what?" Marc asked.

"All that…you know. Show business," Riley said.

"No way," Marc said. "Not when it's your dad. He's a legend."

Riley shrugged.

"So you don't plan to go into the business?" Marc asked.

Riley shook her head. "Not really. I mean, I don't know what I *am* going to do, but I've got time to decide. What about you?"

"I don't know," Marc said. "My dad's sort of a hard act to follow, you know? But I don't have to tell *you* about that."

Riley tried to think of a way to change the subject. But just then she saw Chloe coming towards them. Carrying their drinks.

Oh, no. This is not happening, Riley thought. She jumped up and almost knocked her sister over. "What are you doing here?" she whispered frantically as Chloe tried to keep from spilling the drinks.

"I was just in the back, hanging out with Lennon," Chloe explained. "And he asked me to bring over these drinks."

"Whoa!" Marc said, standing up and staring at Chloe. "Hold on. You…you two look like…wait a minute…Danielle? You've got a twin? How come I've never read about this? Like, anywhere!"

Think fast! Riley told herself. And then she let her mouth take over. "Ooh-la-la, it's just that we've tried to keep it quiet, ever since we found out about each other," she said, babbling. "My sister, Chloe, and I were separated at birth, see, because Mom didn't feel she could raise both of us. So I lived with my father growing up, and Chloe lived with our mother."

"With Faye Huntington?" Marc jumped in. His eyes were rounder than the coffee cups.

"*Oui, oui,*" Riley said, hoping that if she threw in some French he'd fall for this ridiculous story. "And we never even knew each other existed until a few months ago. So now we're together. Isn't it wonderful?" She grabbed Chloe and kissed her on both cheeks – *twice* – as if she hoped that would prove this whole thing was true.

Chloe rubbed at her face to remove the lip gloss.

"Wow." Marc seemed almost speechless. "I can't believe it." He stared at them, amazed, as if he didn't know whether to run to the phone and call the tabloids or to feel lucky that he knew a major secret. "So I'm one of the first people to find out?" he asked, shaking his head in disbelief.

"Yes," Riley said with a sigh. "But you can't tell anyone. You've got to respect our privacy."

"Right," Marc said, nodding. "Okay. I get that. So that's why you didn't want me to know that you're Danielle D'Oisseau."

"Exactly." Riley grabbed at any explanation he'd buy into.

"Wow," he murmured again.

Yeah, Riley thought. Wow. All these lies were exhausting her! "You know what?" she said. "I hate to say this, but I think I should get home. I mean, I have to get up early tomorrow to, um, walk the dog."

"Okay," Marc said, but he sounded disappointed. "But can't you just open that sliding door and let her out? She seems to go out pretty much on her own anyway."

"No, no, we're trying to break her of that habit," Riley said. She took a huge gulp of her cappuccino without sitting down. "So can we go?"

Riley caught Chloe rolling her eyes.

"No problem," Marc said, leaving his coffee behind.

Riley climbed onto his motorbike and put on the helmet. Marc took off, driving through town, towards the beach.

She started to tell him how to get to her house. But then she remembered he knew. Or at least, he *thought* he knew.

Marc drove up to Jacques' beach house and parked his bike. They removed their helmets, and Marc gently brushed some hair out of Riley's eyes.

Then he pulled her into the sweetest kiss she had ever experienced.

66

When the kiss was over, Riley's head was spinning. "So, I guess this is good-bye for now," she said, disappointed now that the date was over.

"Well, maybe not," he said softly. "Do you mind if I come in? I'd really like to meet your dad."

My *dad*? Riley thought. Oh, no! Now what?

chapter
eight

"**Y**ou...you want to come *in*?" Riley said with a lump in her throat.

That's not going to happen, she thought, stalling and trying to think of some excuse to say no.

"Just for a few minutes," Marc said eagerly. "Is it okay?"

What am I going to do? Riley wondered, feeling panicked. She glanced at Jacques' house. Luckily, there weren't too many lights on. "Uh, sorry, but Dad goes to bed very early," she said. "Especially when he's working on a project."

Marc's face fell. "Oh. Well, can I meet him tomorrow? I'm a huge fan."

Riley put her hands on her hips and narrowed her eyes at Marc, pretending to be suspicious. "Hey, what is this? Are you interested in *me*, or are you just using me to meet my dad?" she asked him.

[Riley: Hey, I know it was a dirty trick, but I'm desperate!]

"Oh, no way!" Marc protested quickly. "It's definitely you I want to spend time with. It's just that—"

"What?" Riley said.

"I've been such a big fan of his forever," Marc explained. "I'd love to talk to him about *Tunnel of Rain*."

"Oh, right. The movie he won the Golden Globe for," Riley muttered. "Okay. Yeah, sure. I just don't know when."

Marc tilted his head to one side and gave her a weird smile.

"What?" she asked him.

"Oh, nothing," he replied, still smiling.

Riley shrugged. "Anyway, I'll try to set up a time when you can meet him," she went on. "But it might not happen before you have to go back to New York."

"Okay. No problem," Marc said with that grin pasted on his face. He moved a little closer. Then he leaned in, tilted his head, and kissed her again.

Riley closed her eyes and felt a sweet shiver.

"I had fun tonight," he said.

"Me, too," Riley said. "Too bad you have to go back home so soon." She half meant that. She didn't want to see him go, but at least she wouldn't have to pretend to be French after he was gone.

"By the way," Marc said with another smile. "I'm not going back to New York. I've decided to stay out here and spend the rest of the year with my dad. Isn't that great?"

Great? Yes! Riley thought. I mean, no. Oh, I don't know...

She was so confused! It *would* be great to see Marc all the time, if she could just figure out how to tell him the truth about who she was.

But if she did tell him, would he still like her?

"Yeah," Riley mumbled, feeling like a complete wreck inside. "I'm glad you're staying. Anyway, I've got to go in...uh...the back door. See you sometime."

"When?" Marc called as she walked towards the back of the house.

"I'm not sure," Riley said. "I'll call you."

"You don't have my number!" Marc said. Quickly he took a card out of his wallet, wrote on it, and handed it to her.

"Thanks," Riley said. "Good night." Then she slipped around to the back of Jacques' house and hurried down the beach to her own home. What a mess, she thought. I'm going to have to find a way to tell him the truth – and soon.

But how?

Today is going to be my fresh start at the Newsstand, Chloe decided. Last night she had apologised for making so many silly mistakes, and Lennon had said he was sorry for being so grouchy.

They had cleared the air, and now Chloe was ready to give it her best shot…again.

"Can you put the muffins into the pastry case, Peaches?" Lennon asked in a sweet tone of voice.

"No problem, Dumpling-cheeks!" Chloe said cheerfully.

Lennon laughed.

I'm really going to try today, Chloe decided. She didn't want to get Lennon into any more trouble. And she *definitely* didn't want to get fired now. Not today. It was Thursday, her last possible chance to ask Jacques D'Oisseau for an audition.

The Newsstand would only be open for five more hours. They were closing at two for the auditions.

She glanced at the clock. It was two minutes till nine. Two minutes till Jacques D'Oisseau came in for his coffee and croissant.

Chloe took the large flat tray out of the pastry case and carried it to the back room. She opened a big cardboard box filled with muffins and started piling them on the tray.

But then she heard a voice at the counter. That unmistakable French accent. "*Un café et un croissant*," Jacques said to Cammie, who was at the register.

Chloe rushed out. "I'll make his coffee," she offered, flashing her best smile at Jacques.

"Why, hello!" Jacques said as if he knew her. "I didn't realise you worked here."

71

"I don't," Chloe said, and she heard Cammie snicker. "I mean, I work here, but you're probably thinking of my sister, Riley." Quickly she explained that her twin had shown Jacques the way to the vet.

"Ah," Jacques said, laughing. "Well, it's nice to meet you, Chloe."

"Um, listen." Chloe followed Jacques to his table, carrying his coffee. "May I ask you something?"

"Certainly," Jacques said, gazing at her with mild interest.

Chloe took a deep breath and tried to psych herself up. This seemed like a way-too-bold thing to do. But why not? she told herself. You can't get what you don't ask for!

"I was wondering if I could audition for a small part in the commercial you're shooting," she said finally.

"Well…" Jacques started to shake his head.

"I've done a little acting," Chloe blurted out quickly. "And it won't take much time. Please? I'll make sure we save all the best croissants for your crew," she added as a joke.

Jacques smiled as if he could tell she was trying to charm him. "Oh, why not? You will be here anyway, I suppose, yes?"

"Yes!" Chloe said, happy.

"All right." Jacques nodded. "Be ready at two o'clock when we begin the auditions. I will give you a chance for a screen test, but no promises, okay?"

"Thank you!" Chloe said, reaching out to shake his hand. "Thank you very much!" This is the best! she thought as she hurried back to the counter. "I got it! I got an audition!" she told Cammie, who was ringing up some orders. "And I bet I'll get a part! How hard can it be to play the part of a coffee waitress?"

"Let me answer that for you," a voice from behind her said.

Chloe whirled around and saw Mr. Horner glaring at her, his hands on his hips.

Oops. What did I do now? she wondered.

"For *you*," Mr. Horner said, "playing the part of a coffee waitress seems to be almost impossible!" He glanced at Lennon, who was just coming out of the back room with the tray of muffins in his arms. "I've got an appointment," Mr. Horner said to Lennon. "I expect you to handle this." Then he stomped out of the café.

"Handle what?" Chloe asked Lennon. "What did I do this time?"

"It's what you didn't do," Lennon said. "You left these muffins sitting in the back, so Cammie thought we didn't have any. She told about five customers that we were out of muffins, and they left for Starbucks."

Oh, boy, Chloe thought, covering her face.

"Just get to work," Lennon snapped.

Chloe tried not to make any more mistakes all morning. But it was hard, with Lennon watching her like a hawk. She kept wondering when she was going to spill something, make the wrong drink, or get yelled at for what she called "being friendly with the customers" but Lennon called "gabbing on the job."

I'll hang on until two o'clock, Chloe decided. Then I'll quit, and Lennon can stop worrying about my messing up all the time. And I'll have the chance to audition for the commercial.

Tara came in at one-forty-five and ordered a mocha.

"We're closing in fifteen minutes," Chloe said, excited.

Jacques and the video crew had already started to arrive. Chloe quickly served them the coffees they ordered.

"Did you talk Jacques into an audition?" Tara asked.

"Yes! But I haven't had a minute to get ready for it!" Chloe confided. She stirred syrup into Tara's drink and handed it to her.

"Just act natural," Tara coached her. "Be yourself and don't stare at the camera – unless they tell you to, of course. But act as if the camera loves you." Tara took a sip of her mocha and almost spit it out. "Yuck! You put raspberry syrup in this instead of chocolate!" She shoved the drink back towards Chloe, behind the counter.

Lennon came over, shaking his head. "Okay, that's it," he said. "I'm sorry, Chloe, but you're fired."

"What?" Chloe's eyes popped open wide. Was he kidding? "It's just Tara's drink! You can't fire me for that!"

"Thanks a lot!" Tara snapped.

"It's *not* just Tara's drink," Lennon said. "You're a *terrible* waitress. You messed up the last four coffees for the crew!"

Chloe glanced over at the video crew. Some of them were watching her. And so were the other actresses who had arrived for the audition. They looked like supermodels – tall, thin, and totally gorgeous.

Oh, great! she thought as she took off her apron and tossed it onto the counter. Now I look like an idiot in front of everyone!

"Thanks a lot, Lennon." She brushed past him to run to the rest room. But in her rush she knocked over a half-empty cardboard cup of cold coffee. It spilled down the front of her jeans. "Oh, no!" Chloe cried, totally upset and desperate to get out of sight. The whole roomful of film people turned to stare at her. A few of them snickered.

Don't cry, she told herself as she pushed into the rest room to hide. Don't cry. Whatever you do, don't cry.

For a minute she just buried her face in her hands. Then she splashed her cheeks with water.

"Chloe? They're calling for you out front," Cammie said, poking her head into the rest room.

Okay, Chloe decided, still shaking inside. I can do this. She brushed her hair, wiped off her jeans, put on some lip gloss and hurried to do her audition.

By the time she came out of the rest room, Jacques' crew had set up lights. They were getting ready to shoot the first screen tests.

"All right, everyone," Jacques said to the collection of actresses. Chloe hurried to join them. "We are auditioning for speaking and nonspeaking parts today. So please just stand in front of the camera, tell me your name, and give us a little bit about your acting experience. Then please read the lines from this script, okay?"

That should be easy enough, Chloe thought. But she was still shaking inside. And so embarrassed she wanted to hide.

She watched as the first actress did her audition.

"Hi, my name is Inga," the model-actress said. "I'm five-eleven, I weigh a hundred and twenty pounds, and my special talents are mime, ballet dancing and luge." She went on to list all the commercials she'd been in. Then she read the script. She had a cute Scandinavian accent.

Wow, Chloe thought. She's so tall and beautiful!

"Very nice," Jacques said, but Riley saw the other crew people shaking their heads.

"She doesn't sound very real," someone whispered.

"She doesn't even sound American!" someone else said.

"All right, let's see who's next. Chloe?" Jacques motioned to her.

Already? Chloe swallowed hard. She didn't want to have to go on so soon. Her stomach was still turning somersaults, and the stain on her jeans was still wet.

She stepped in front of the camera and smiled. "Hi, my name is Chloe Carlson, but you know that already, right? Because, I mean, I just told you this afternoon."

Someone in the background giggled.

My voice is shaking! Chloe realised. I sound like a porpoise with laryngitis, and I'm not even singing!

"Go on," Jacques said. "Tell us something about yourself."

"Um, yeah." Chloe nodded. "Well, I work here in the Newsstand, or at least I did until recently. So I'm very familiar with coffee. And I've done a lot of acting in, uh...school plays."

"Really?" Jacques smiled and tried to look encouraging. "Like what?"

"Well, I got really good reviews in junior high," Chloe said. "I played Woodstock in *You're a Good Man, Charlie Brown*."

The cameraman out-and-out laughed. Some of the actresses giggled, too.

I'm blowing this! Chloe thought. What did I say? I'm very familiar with coffee? Just shoot me now!

She glanced at Lennon, who was standing in the back watching. He had his arms crossed over his chest and was covering his face with one hand.

"That is good," Jacques said. "Can you read the first page of the script?"

"I think so," Chloe said. She picked it up and read. "'If I don't get a latte, I'm going to do something I'll forget,'" she said. "I mean, '*regret.*' Sorry. I read that wrong. Can I do it again?"

"No need," Jacques said. "That was fine. Please leave your résumé and head shot with Patty."

Résumé? Head shot? "I don't have those," Chloe blurted out, and the crew smiled again.

"Well, I'm sorry, Chloe," Jacques said, "but I think we are looking for someone with a little more experience."

"Okay." Chloe wished she could disappear through the floor. This is mortifying, she thought. And it was all Lennon's fault. If he hadn't fired me mere minutes before I had to go on, I would have done a better job! She ran towards the back room. Anything to get out of there.

Lennon followed her. "Are you okay?" he asked.

"What do you care? You made me look bad!" she said, her voice still shaking.

"Well, you served four lattes without any milk!" he shot back.

"But that's not a reason to fire me right before my audition! You ruined my chance to be in this commercial!" she said, her voice rising.

"Hey, don't blame me," Lennon said. "You ruined *that* all by yourself."

Whoa. Chloe was shocked. Did he really say that to her? "Don't you even care one bit whether I get this acting job?" Chloe asked.

"Sure," Lennon said. "About as much as you care whether I keep *my* job."

Chloe's throat closed up. She thought she might cry. "Don't worry. I won't mess up your life anymore," she said sharply. "I'm leaving!"

"Good!" Lennon cried.

Chloe grabbed her backpack and stomped out the back door of the café. But as soon as she was outside, she felt terrible.

Why did I yell at Lennon? she thought. It's not his fault that I messed up my job. Or my audition.

Then a horrible thought hit her – right in the gut.

Wait a minute. What *really* happened back there?

Did I just lose my job, or did I lose my boyfriend, too?

chapter
nine

"**W**ait, wait, tell me again," Riley said to Chloe late that afternoon. The two of them were sprawled on their beds, eating pieces of melon. "What did he say *exactly*?"

"Who? Jacques or Lennon?" Chloe asked.

"Lennon," Riley answered. "Did he say he never wanted to see you again?"

"No," Chloe admitted. "But he made it pretty clear he never wanted to see me *make coffee* again."

"Yeah, I get that part," Riley said. "Manuelo pretty much feels the same way."

Chloe tried to laugh, but it came out more like a moan.

"And Jacques never wants to see you again, either, I'm guessing?" Riley asked.

"Hey, I thought you were trying to cheer me up!" Chloe protested.

"Okay, okay, sorry." Riley thought for a minute. "So

my advice would be, call Lennon and ask him what he meant."

"Call him and say 'Excuse me, but did we just break up?' No way. Too embarrassing. And anyway, what if he says yes?"

"Yeah, that would hurt," Riley had to admit. She took another bite of melon and shook her head. "I don't know, Chloe. Maybe you should ask someone else for advice. I haven't exactly been acing my own social life these days."

"What's wrong?" Chloe asked.

Riley quickly explained what had happened on her date with Marc. "And he's not leaving town at the end of the week," she said.

"But that's great!" Chloe said. "Isn't it? I mean, I thought he was someone you could really like."

"He is." Riley nodded. "But what's he going to think when he finds out I'm not connected to show business? And not French? And not even a little bit famous? Plus he wants me to introduce him to Jacques. The whole thing's a huge mess."

"Yeah, that's bad," Chloe admitted. "Well, you were in the West Malibu High School talent show last year," she joked. "Do you think that counts as a show business connection?"

Riley didn't even bother to answer that. "This is serious!" she said. "What am I going to do?"

Chloe sat up as if she'd just got a brilliant idea. "How about this? Jacques comes into the Newsstand every morning at nine for coffee," she said. "Maybe you could make a date with Marc to meet him there at nine."

"What good will that do?" Riley asked.

"When Marc comes in, you tell him the truth about who you are, because you have to do that anyway, right?" Chloe said. "But then right away you offer to introduce him to Jacques. I mean, Jacques will be sitting right there and you *do* know him, right?"

Hmm. Not a bad plan, Riley thought. Jacques was so nice. He would probably be fine about talking to Marc for a few minutes.

"But what about the fact that Marc's dad is a superstar, and Marc said he'd never hang with someone who's not involved in show business?" Riley worried.

Chloe shrugged. "You've got to tell him sometime," she pointed out.

True, Riley thought. She went to the phone and dialled the number Marc had given her.

"Can you meet me tomorrow morning at nine at the Newsstand?" she said when he answered.

"Sure, what's up?" Marc asked.

Riley hesitated for a moment, then she said, "I have something important to tell you."

Riley dragged herself out of bed early Friday morning, considering that there was no school, and got to the Newsstand by eight forty-five.

"Hi," Lennon said, hurrying past her with two coffees in his hands as she walked in.

"Hi," Riley said and immediately went into supersensitive mode, trying to figure out exactly what his "Hi" meant.

[Riley: I pride myself on being able to read whole chapters into a single syllable, you know? What girl doesn't? So when Lennon said "Hi," I ran through a whole list of possibilities. Was it, "Hi, I wish you were Chloe instead of Riley so I could make up with you"? Or did he mean, "You look exactly like the girl I'm totally over, so get out of my sight"? Or was it just, "Hi, I hope you're not as down on me as your sister is and, by the way, could you be careful not to spill anything, either"? But none of those sounded right. Finally I had to admit that he might have just been trying to say hello. Call me crazy, but it could be true!]

She ordered a cappuccino and hovered around the counter, waiting for Jacques. At nine on the dot he walked in, ordered his coffee and croissant, and sat down with *Le Monde*.

"Hi," Riley said, approaching him with her cappuccino in hand.

"Oh, hello," Jacques said. "Riley, right?"

Riley nodded. "Um, Monsieur D'Oisseau, there's something I wanted to ask you." She cleared her throat. "Would you mind if I sat down for a minute?"

"Please," Jacques said, gesturing grandly to the chair across from him. He even stood up and held the chair for her. "I am forever in your debt for rescuing my petite Chaudette. How can I return the favour?"

That's a tricky one, Riley thought. She had spent half of last night trying to figure out how to tell Jacques that she'd been pretending to be his daughter. But there just didn't seem to be a good way to say it. Finally she had decided to just start at the beginning and tell him the whole story.

"Do you remember last weekend when I helped you find the vet?" Riley began.

"But of course," Jacques said, smiling warmly at her.

"Well…" Riley took a deep breath. She was just about to plunge into the details when the door opened and Marc walked in. Whoops! Riley thought. I should have told him to come later.

"Hi!" Marc said, beaming when he saw her sitting with Jacques.

"Oh, no," Riley mumbled. In a panic, she tried to think of some way to blurt out the whole truth quickly.

Marc rushed over to their table and stuck out his hand. "Monsieur D'Oisseau! It's so nice to meet you," he said. "You have a delightful daughter."

"Oh!" Jacques looked totally surprised as he shook Marc's hand. "You've met Danielle?"

"But of course!" Marc said. *"La jeune fille qui vous accompagne m'a dit qu'elle est Danielle."*

Whoa! They're going to speak French, Riley thought. That's not fair!

"Mais, non!" Jacques said, answering quickly in French. Then he rattled off about five more sentences that Riley didn't understand, and Marc did the same thing.

What a nightmare! Riley thought. She knew they were talking about her, or rather, Danielle. But she had no idea what they were saying! Riley watched their faces.

[**Riley**: I know what you're thinking, so don't even say it. Now would be a good time to be able to read whole paragraphs into a few syllables, right? Yeah. I wish!]

The conversation went on in French for another few minutes.

Finally Jacques stood up with his coffee and paper and walked towards the door. *"Au revoir,"* he called to Riley.

Marc started to follow him.

"Hey! Where are you going?" Riley said. She was just about to tell them both the whole truth! Now her chance was slipping away.

"Your father offered me a job as a production assistant," Marc replied. "So I've got to go. But I have something important to tell you, too. I'll see

85

you tomorrow at the shoot, okay? You're coming, right?"

Coming to the shoot? Uh, no. She wasn't invited. In fact, she knew that the Newsstand would be closed to the public all day tomorrow.

But if Marc was going to be there, and if he wanted to tell her something, she'd have to find a way to get in.

"Sure. See you tomorrow," Riley called as Marc walked out the door.

chapter
ten

"**H**ave another muffin," Manuelo said, trying to cheer up Chloe. "They're still warm from the oven."

Chloe flopped onto the couch and sighed. "My life is a mess, Manuelo. Another muffin isn't going to help."

"It can't hurt," he said, carrying the plate over and leaving it on the coffee table.

Chloe shook her head and went to the freezer. "I'm going to need something stronger," she joked as she took out a pint of ice cream and fished around for a spoon. Then she flopped back onto the couch and picked up the phone.

There's got to be *someone* I can talk to! she thought. Other than Manuelo. Someone who can tell me what to do about Lennon.

She dialled Tara's number and got her answering machine.

Then she tried Quinn. Same thing.

Amanda was third on her speed dial. Luckily, she picked up on the third ring.

"Hi," Chloe said. "You doing anything?"

"Just sitting by the phone, waiting for your next call," Amanda joked.

"Oh, come on," Chloe said. "I haven't called you *that* many times."

"Every half hour since ten this morning," Amanda said. "Have you heard from Lennon yet?"

"Not yet," Chloe said. "That's what's driving me crazy! I can't stand the suspense."

"So call him!" Amanda advised. "If you'd done it three hours ago the way I told you to, you'd at least know where you stand with him."

Chloe thought about it. Amanda was probably right. She should just call Lennon and ask him whether he'd meant to break up with her or not.

It was totally reasonable. But Chloe couldn't do it. "I guess I have too much pride or something."

"Listen, I hate to say it, but I was just heading out the door," Amanda said. "My mom's taking me to the mall."

"Fine." Chloe caved in. "I'll let you go."

What choice did she have? If there was one rule she and her friends stuck to, it was "Never interfere with a shopping trip."

"I'll talk to you later," Amanda promised.

That's okay, Chloe thought. Besides, I think I just heard Riley come home.

She could always count on Riley for sympathy.

Chloe hung up and waited for her sister to appear in the living room.

"Do I smell muffins?" Riley asked, looking almost as miserable as Chloe felt.

Uh-oh, Chloe thought. Looks like Riley needs sympathy almost as much as I do! "On the table," she said, pointing. "But I've moved on to the ice cream. You want a spoon?"

"No thanks." Riley took a muffin, stared at it, and put it back down.

"Wow," Chloe said. "You must have had a *really* bad day. What happened?"

Riley told her about her coffee date with Marc and Jacques.

"They spoke French for five whole minutes?" Chloe asked, her eyes wide.

Riley nodded. "And I never got a chance to confess that I'm not Danielle."

"I'm betting Jacques already knows that," Chloe teased.

"You know what I mean." Riley covered her face with her hands. "And then Marc said he had something to tell me, which he'll do tomorrow at the shoot. So I've got to get in there somehow. Do you think Lennon—"

"I haven't talked to him since he fired me," Chloe interrupted, shaking her head.

"Oh." Riley nodded.

"But don't think I'm all alone without Lennon," Chloe said, digging into the ice cream container. "Oh, no. I'll be perfectly fine. I still have my friends, Ben and Jerry."

"They're my friends, too," Riley said, standing up to get herself a spoon.

The phone rang. Chloe grabbed it and checked the Caller ID. Her face lit up. It was Lennon!

"Hello?" she said, answering the phone.

"Um, hi," he said. "It's me. I was wondering...can you meet me somewhere so we can talk?"

"Definitely!" Chloe was happy just to hear his voice. But then she froze. What did he want to talk about? Was he going to break up with her – officially? "Where and when?" she asked.

"You pick the place," he said. "Anywhere but the Newsstand."

Yeah, I'll bet, she thought. You don't want to be seen with me there ever again!

Chloe chose California Dream, the beach café just a few blocks from her house. She promised to meet him in an hour, leaving just enough time to change her clothes three times and fix her hair twice.

When she walked in, Lennon was already there, sitting in the booth he knew was her favourite – the one by the windows.

She tried to read the look on his face, but she couldn't. Was he going to dump her? Yell at her? Or was he just waiting to see if she'd apologise?

"Hi," he said, sounding as if he wasn't sure how to act. "I didn't know what you wanted to eat, so I didn't order yet."

"Just a glass of water for me," she said.

Lennon motioned to the waitress and ordered one water and one iced tea.

Then he reached across the table and took her hands. "Listen, I'm really sorry for what happened yesterday," he said. "I was just under so much pressure. Mr. Horner was hammering me, and I lost it. But I really didn't want to fire you right before your audition and in front of everybody. I'm sorry if I embarrassed you. Or if that made you mess up."

He's so sweet! Chloe thought. She let out a sigh of relief, totally grateful that Lennon was saying all the right things.

"I'm sorry, too," she said, squeezing his hands to show how much she meant it. "I mean, I was a totally awful coffee waitress."

"Yeah, you were," Lennon admitted with a laugh.

"I know." Chloe covered her face. "No milk in the lattes? That *was* bad, wasn't it?"

Lennon smiled.

"Anyway, I'm really sorry for acting like I thought you should cover for me on the job," she went on. "And it's not your fault that I didn't get a part in that commercial, either. I wasn't up to the competition."

"You'd be good in a paper towel commercial," Lennon joked. "You've got a lot of experience. You know, wiping up spilled coffee?"

"Very funny." Chloe yanked her hands away, pretending to be mad. But she liked the way he teased her. It was his way of showing how much he appreciated her in *spite* of her faults. "There's only one thing I really wish," she added.

"What?" Lennon asked.

"It would be so cool to hang out and watch them shoot that commercial tomorrow," she said. "Is there any way you could sneak me and Riley in?"

"Done," Lennon said.

"Really?" Chloe asked. "Are you sure?"

"Yup. I already thought of that, so I asked Mr. Horner," Lennon explained. "He said it was okay as long as you don't touch anything or try to make any coffee."

"You got it," Chloe said. She was so happy that she and Lennon had made up. And there were three whole days of winter break left, too! Maybe she could still salvage this disastrous week after all!

"How do I look?" Sierra asked Riley that night at the Voodoo Lounge.

The two of them stood in the rest room, where Sierra had got dressed in her black leather trousers and red chiffon top with wild, torn sleeves. She twisted a hunk of her wavy red hair into a knot on the side of her head, letting the rest flow free.

"You look amazing, as usual," Riley said. "Are you psyched about tonight?"

"Totally," Sierra said. "A*nd* scared. I mean, I want my parents to find out the truth about my band, and I told them to come. But I'm terrified about it, too."

"I know what you mean," Riley said. "That's how I felt about telling Marc that I'm not Danielle."

"But you *didn't* tell him!" Sierra scolded. "You bailed! What about our pact?"

"We said we'd come clean by the end of the week," Riley argued. "I still have time left."

Sierra opened the rest room door a crack and peeked out. "Wow. The place is jammed!" she said. "You'd better hurry if you want to get a good table."

"Chloe and Lennon and Tara and Quinn are saving me a seat," Riley said. "But yeah, I'd better go before someone steals the chair. Anyway, break a leg."

"Thanks." Sierra pulled on a pair of high, spiky black leather boots. Then she turned to the mirror to add some eyeliner and fuss with her makeup.

Riley pushed out through the crowd of high school and college kids who had packed the Voodoo Lounge. The club was mostly dark, with coloured lights aimed at the walls in various places.

Indie rock music was pulsing on the sound system while the crowd waited for The Wave to come on.

"Hi!" Riley said, giving Chloe a hug and squeezing into a chair at the crowded table.

She looks so happy! Riley thought. Then she wondered, Can Marc and I ever be as good together as Chloe and Lennon?

Most of the band members were already onstage, getting ready to start playing. Riley gazed at Alex Zimmer, the guitar player she had gone out with for a while. She hadn't talked to him much in the past few weeks, and now she knew why. He was really sweet, and she liked him a lot. But he wasn't as funny or interesting as Marc Hudson. And she didn't feel as if she could totally be herself with him, the way she did with Marc.

That's funny, Riley thought. I feel like I can be myself with Marc, but he thinks I'm someone else!

Finally Sierra came out of the rest room and jumped up onto the stage.

Alex took the microphone. "Hi, everyone. Thanks for coming out tonight," he said in his quiet, shy way. "We're going to kick this off with a song our bass player wrote, called 'Memory Morning.' Give it up, everybody, for Sierra!"

The crowd cheered and applauded, and the band launched into the first song. It was amazing, a really driving beat with a wonderful melody and excellent lyrics.

The Wave is so incredibly awesome, Riley thought. How could Sierra's parents possibly be disappointed if they saw her now?

Riley looked around the packed club, hoping to spot the Pomeroys in the crowd. But they hadn't shown up.

The next three songs were awesome, too. Saul, the drummer, sang on the last one. A bunch of people, including Tara and Quinn, got up and started dancing, so Riley joined them.

When Saul's song was over, Sierra took the microphone.

"We've got a brand-new song that we're going to try out for you tonight," she said. "It was written by our keyboard player, Marta. She really wanted to sing it for you herself, but for her own safety – and yours – we talked her out of it."

Everyone laughed.

"So anyway, Alex and I are going to try to do your song justice, Marta," Sierra said, shooting a smile towards the keyboard player. "This is 'Random Access Misery.'"

Sierra strummed the first chords, Saul kicked off the drum riff, and they launched into it.

"Wow," Chloe said, leaning over halfway through the song. "What a great song, huh? Sierra sounds awesome!"

"Yeah," Riley said. "I wish Sierra's mom could hear her."

Chloe glanced at the door, which was behind Riley's shoulder. "Looks like you got your wish," she said.

so little time

Riley whirled around and saw Sierra's parents. They had just come in and were standing near the entrance watching, their eyes wide. It seemed as if they couldn't believe what they were seeing.

Sierra sang the last lines:

"Want to live, want to be
Someone who looks just like me,
But can't let go of the memories
From my random access misery."

The crowd cheered and hooted when the song was over, and Sierra took a jumping-up-and-down bow.

"Thanks, everyone!" she shouted. "We're going to take a break now, but don't go away. We've still got a long night ahead!" Then she put down her guitar and hopped off the stage.

Riley darted out of her seat and ran over to Sierra. "Your parents came!" she said, shouting to be heard above the music playing over the sound system.

"I see them," Sierra said. "They're right behind you."

Riley stepped back to make room for the Pomeroys. She held her breath. What are they going to do? she wondered.

As soon as they could reach Sierra through the crowd, Mr. And Mrs. Pomeroy rushed forward to hug her.

"Honey, that was wonderful!" her mother said. "I had no idea!"

"I'm amazed!" her father added. "Totally shocked but so proud! Your band is really good!"

Sierra beamed. "Thanks," she said, grinning. "So you don't mind if I'm in a band like this?"

"No, of course not," her mother said. "As long as it doesn't interfere with your violin practice."

"And we can see that it hasn't," her father added. "After all, you won that statewide competition last week."

"Right!" Sierra said, so happy she looked as if she might explode.

"There's only one thing," her mother said, stepping back and frowning a little. She looked Sierra up and down. "What on earth are you wearing? What happened to the button-down shirt and checked jumper you had on when you left home this afternoon?"

Oops. Riley glanced at Sierra, waiting to see what she'd do. But Sierra didn't miss a beat.

"Oh, this? This is Riley's!" she lied. "I'd *never* own anything as wild as this! Riley made me borrow it for the concert, so I'd look, you know, more like a rock star."

Mrs. Pomeroy glanced at Riley. "Well, I'm sorry, Riley, but I think it's a bit too much," she said.

"Oh, right, I see that," Sierra agreed quickly. "Too much. Definitely "

Oh, well. Riley sighed. At least Sierra told them the truth about her band. That was a good start.

Now it was Riley's turn to tell the truth.

To Marc. Tomorrow. No matter what!

chapter
eleven

"I don't believe this!" Riley gasped the next morning, standing outside the Newsstand. "The place is crawling with people. We can't even get to the front door!"

"Lennon said we should go in the back door," Chloe said, leading the way around the corner to the alley.

Good thing, Riley thought. Because with all the trucks parked out in front and the production people guarding the front door, they'd never get in the regular way.

They hurried to the back door and found Lennon waiting for them.

"Hi." He let them in. "Mr. Horner said it's okay for you to be here as long as you stay out of the way."

Inside, Lennon put his arms around Chloe's waist and gave her a hug.

"Am I out of the way back here with you?" Chloe asked with a grin.

"See you guys later," Riley called, leaving them alone. She was on a mission. Today the truth was going to come out – whether Marc liked it or not!

She headed into the coffee shop and found the place crawling with video crew people. Lights and electrical wires were everywhere. She had to watch her step to keep from tripping over metal equipment cases.

"Hi, Danielle," someone said as she squeezed past a light stand.

Huh? Riley's head whipped around. Who said that? she wondered. These people were all complete strangers!

"Hey, Danielle," another crew member said. "You looking for your dad? He's right over there." She pointed to the far side of the coffee shop. To Jacques.

Whoa! Riley thought. What's going on?

Her heart started pounding, and she scanned the room for Marc. There he is, Riley thought. Over near the windows, talking to Jacques. She edged past the camera and cameraman, trying not to bump into anything.

"Hi, Danielle," the cameraman said to her. "You're looking perky today."

What's going on? Riley wanted to shout.

But then Jacques spotted her, and his face lit up. He rushed towards her. "Danielle!" He took her face in his hands and kissed her on both cheeks. "Good morning, my darling daughter!"

Everyone in the room stopped working for a moment. They were all quiet, watching her.

Riley didn't know what to say. She hesitated for a minute. "Dad?" she finally mumbled in a weak voice.

The whole crew burst out laughing.

And Marc laughed the hardest. "Hi, Riley," he said, taking her by the arm and pulling her aside.

"What?" Riley was totally confused. "You know my real name?"

"Yeah," he said with a grin. "I've been on to you for two days now."

Riley was dumbfounded. She stared at him, hoping he'd explain it because she was so surprised, she couldn't think of the right questions to ask.

"You should see the look on your face!" Marc said. He led her off to a corner away from the crew. Everyone else went back to work.

"But how did you find out?" Riley finally managed to say.

"When I dropped you off at Jacques' house after the movie," Marc explained, "you gave yourself away. You said your dad had won the Golden Globe award for *Tunnel of Rain*."

"Didn't he?" Riley asked.

"Nope." Marc shook his head. "Faye Huntington won for best actress in the picture. But she gave the award to Jacques out of gratitude for all his help and support directing her in the film."

"Oops," Riley said.

"Somehow I thought Jacques and Faye's daughter would know that," Marc kidded her.

Duh! Riley covered her face. No wonder he had given her such a strange smile that night! Then she remembered something. "What about yesterday?" she asked, still trying to figure this all out. "When you came in here and you were talking to Jacques in French…"

"I called you Danielle in front of him," Marc admitted. "But in French I told him the whole story. That you were pretending to be his daughter. He thought it was funny, and he liked the fact that I spoke French. So he offered me a job on the shoot."

Well, I'm glad someone thinks it's funny! Riley thought.

"It was Jacques' idea to pull this stunt on you," Marc said, still smiling. "And I figured you deserved it, since you've been basically living a lie all week."

"But I tried to tell you the truth!" Riley protested. "On the beach, remember?"

"Yeah, I know." Marc looked sort of sorry. "I should have believed you, too." His face was serious now, and Riley's heart sank.

"So I guess I know what you wanted to tell me," she said. "I mean, you made it pretty clear that you don't want to go out with an average girl."

"That's right, I don't," Marc said. He stared at her for a minute. "I want to go out with *you*."

Huh? Riley was stunned silent.

"There's nothing average about you, Riley," Marc said, and those dimples of his kicked into high gear.

Aw, Riley thought. That was so nice!

"How about tonight?" Marc asked. "A movie, maybe?"

"I'd love to," Riley said, thrilled. This was working out better than expected! "But there's just one thing."

"What?" Marc asked.

"Promise me I don't have to speak a word of French!"

chapter
twelve

"**S**he's terrible!" Chloe whispered to Lennon. "She's gorgeous, but she can't act!"

The two of them stood behind the counter, watching the video shoot in the Newsstand. Jacques had been shooting take after take of just one scene from the coffee commercial.

"Look at her!" Chloe whispered to Riley. "She keeps serving that coffee as if it's a diamond ring on a pillow or something."

"It's true," Lennon agreed. "Even *you* would have been better in the part."

"Thanks...I think," Chloe said. She wasn't sure if he was teasing her or not.

"Quiet!" Jacques said, clapping his hands to silence the crew. "This is not working. We are supposed to be at the Newsstand, and there isn't a single newspaper in sight."

Marc grabbed some newspapers from the wall

rack and spread them out on the table. "Does that help?" he asked.

"Yes," Jacques said. "No. I don't know." He threw up his hands. "This whole scene is wrong!"

He took the actress aside and talked to her, gesturing rapidly as if he was unhappy with her performance.

I'd hate to be in her place, Chloe thought.

Jacques looked around the room. He seemed to want something. Then he motioned to Chloe. "Um, excuse me? Could you come here for a moment?"

"Me?" Chloe froze.

Jacques nodded. "You auditioned for me, didn't you?"

"Yes," Chloe replied.

"Well, good. We need you, so here's your big chance," he said.

"Seriously?" Chloe's face lit up. I can't believe it! she thought. I *knew* I could do a better job than that actress! She shot a glance at Lennon and Riley, and they both smiled back.

"Great!" Chloe said. "But what do you want me to wear? Am I dressed okay for the part of the waitress?"

"The waitress?" Jacques said with a small smile. "Oh, no. I have something else for you." He led her over to the table where they were shooting the scene.

"Derek? This is Chloe. Chloe, Derek," Jacques said, introducing her to the actor who was playing a customer.

"So am I going to be another customer?" Chloe wondered out loud.

Jacques picked up the newspapers that were spread on Derek's table.

"Yes. Chloe, I want you to sit at the table right behind Derek," Jacques said. "So I can see you in the shot. But you'll be reading this newspaper."

"Is that it?" she asked. "That's my part?"

Jacques nodded. "I am sure you'll be wonderful in it," he said with a kind smile.

Okay. At least I'm *in* the commercial! Chloe thought, still excited. But the minute she sat down and picked up the newspaper, Jacques clapped his hands.

"No, no," he called to her. "Hold up the paper higher. Higher. Higher, please. There!"

"But you can't even see my face now!" Chloe cried out from behind the paper.

"It's perfect!" Jacques said. "Action!"

Oh, well, Chloe thought. At least I'm in show business!

Five takes later they were finished with that scene. Chloe watched the playback on the video monitor. Just as she thought, her face was totally blocked by the newspaper.

"Well, at least I can tell people, 'Those are my hands!'" she said, and everyone laughed.

When the shoot was over, a production assistant gave Chloe a cheque for one hundred dollars.

"Wow!" Chloe was amazed. "Pretty good money for just holding up a newspaper!" She turned to Riley and the two guys. "You want to go out to dinner? My treat."

"I've already got dinner covered," Lennon said, leading her outside.

Riley and Marc followed.

When they reached the street, Chloe saw two motor scooters parked at the curb. One was Marc's, she knew. But the other?

"What's up?" she asked, turning to Lennon.

"It's just one of three things I wanted to do during this break," he said. "I rented this bike so I could teach you how to ride it."

"Aw! That's so nice!" Chloe said. "You remembered!" She gave him a hug. "But what are the other two things?"

"Well, I thought we could drive to the beach – all four of us," Lennon said. "And make a fire and roast hot dogs and marshmallows while we listen to nothing but songs with *fire* in the title."

I don't believe it! Chloe thought. He was listening the whole time!

Lennon flipped open the lid on the carrier on the back of his scooter. Inside were hot dogs, marshmallows, drinks and crisps. "See?" he said. "Dinner!"

Chloe wanted to melt. "And what's the third thing?" she asked, feeling all warm and toasty inside.

"This," he said, pulling her towards him and giving her a long kiss. "I'm off for the rest of the weekend. Let's get out of here."

Hey, Chloe thought. That works for me!

so little time

Chloe
and Riley's

SCRAPBOOK

so little time

Check out book 12!

best friends forever

How did this happen? Chloe wondered. This morning, we were all best friends, now some of us aren't speaking to the rest of us.

And why? Because we couldn't agree on how to handle our Business Studies team project. You would think coming up with a cool product and selling it would be fun and easy. But it's not.

Not when two people want to be in charge.

After the big fight, Sierra had taken sides with Tara. The two of them had decided to form their own team. And they took their product idea with them. They were going to make and sell the Spiral Bracelet by themselves.

Larry had decided to stick with Team Carlson. "I'm not deserting you at a time like this," Larry had said – not to Chloe, but to Riley. He'd had a crush on Riley since forever. "Don't worry. We're still the best."

The best? The best at what? Chloe wondered. We don't have a product any more!

And that wasn't even the worst of it.

Next Saturday night was the Master Crush concert. The Master Crush concert that she, Chloe Carlson, wanted to go to more than any other concert on the planet.

Last week Tara had scored two tickets from her father, who had major connections, and offered one to Chloe. But then, after the fight this morning, Tara had taken her offer back. "We are so not going to this concert together. Not after this!" she had announced to Chloe.

Now what? Chloe wondered. She sat down at her computer and logged on to the Web. She typed in: MASTER CRUSH TICKETS, MALIBU.

A bunch of ads popped up. They were ads for tickets to the Master Crush concert! Chloe felt a rush of hope.

And then her hope collapsed like a bad hairstyle on a rainy day. She read the fine print.

SINGLE TIX MASTER CRUSH $500 OR BEST OFFER

PAIR TIX MASTER CRUSH 10TH ROW $1000

Five hundred dollars? A thousand dollars?

Chloe's head was spinning. How was she ever going to score a ticket to the hottest concert of the century?

mary-kateandashley

TWO of a kind ™

(1)	It's a Twin Thing	(0 00 714480 6)
(2)	How to Flunk Your First Date	(0 00 714479 2)
(3)	The Sleepover Secret	(0 00 714478 4)
(4)	One Twin Too Many	(0 00 714477 6)
(5)	To Snoop or Not to Snoop	(0 00 714476 8)
(6)	My Sister the Supermodel	(0 00 714475 X)
(7)	Two's a Crowd	(0 00 714474 1)
(8)	Let's Party	(0 00 714473 3)
(9)	Calling All Boys	(0 00 714472 5)
(10)	Winner Take All	(0 00 714471 7)
(11)	PS Wish You Were Here	(0 00 714470 9)
(12)	The Cool Club	(0 00 714469 5)
(13)	War of the Wardrobes	(0 00 714468 7)
(14)	Bye-Bye Boyfriend	(0 00 714467 9)
(15)	It's Snow Problem	(0 00 714466 0)

HarperCollins*Entertainment*

PARACHUTE PRESS

DUALSTAR PUBLICATIONS

AOL

mary-kateandashley.com
AOL Keyword: mary-kateandashley

TM & © 2002 Dualstar Entertainment Group, LLC.

mary-kate and ashley

TWO of a kind ™

(16)	Likes Me, Likes Me Not	(0 00 714465 2)
(17)	Shore Thing	(0 00 714464 4)
(18)	Two for the Road	(0 00 714463 6)
(19)	Surprise, Surprise!	(0 00 714462 8)
(20)	Sealed with a Kiss	(0 00 714461 X)
(21)	Now you see him, Now you don't	(0 00 714446 6)
(22)	April Fool's Rules	(0 00 714460 1)
(23)	Island Girls	(0 00 714445 8)
(24)	Surf Sand and Secrets	(0 00 714459 8)
(25)	Closer Than Ever	(0 00 715881 5)
(26)	The Perfect Gift	(0 00 715882 3)
(27)	The Facts About Flirting	(0 00 715883 1)

HarperCollins*Entertainment*

PARACHUTE PRESS

DUALSTAR PUBLICATIONS

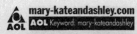
mary-kateandashley.com
AOL Keyword: mary-kateandashley

mary-kateandashley

Sweet 16

(1) *Never Been Kissed*   (0 00 714879 8)
(2) *Wishes and Dreams*   (0 00 714880 1)
(3) *The Perfect Summer*   (0 00 714881 X)

HarperCollins*Entertainment*

PARACHUTE PRESS

DUALSTAR PUBLICATIONS

mary-kateandashley.com
AOL Keyword: mary-kateandashley

LOG ON!

mary-kateandashley.com
AOL Keyword: mary-kateandashley

DUALSTAR
ONLINE

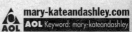